The Heart Shed

by

Kevin Cobb

Printed in the United States of America

First Printing, 2018

ISBN 13: 978-1981231386
ISBN 10: 1981231382

The Heart Shed

by

Kevin Cobb

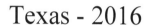

Texas - 2016

Chapter 1

"Pneumonia?" asked Steve Dunham.

"Yes," said Dr. Manchester, pointing at a chest x-ray. "See these infiltrates, these large white patches throughout your lungs? That's pneumonia."

Steve's eyes widened.

"I'll give you antibiotics. You'll take the week off, enjoy some TV and napping. You could be back to school by next week."

"I can't," said Steve between coughs. "Exams are coming up. I can't miss it."

"The school will get a sub," Dr. Manchester urged. "Take this time to rest. You could still return before exams get started. Come back Friday. If your lungs are clear, you could be back to work Monday."

"No way," said Steve. "Of course I need to prepare my finals for next week, but I'm talking about my final as a

1

student. I'm taking a PhD class. I have my own final this Friday."

Dr. Manchester's perpetual smile flattened. He stroked his white manicured beard, and his cheerful demeanor turned somber. "Steven, you could die from this. Pneumonia is serious."

Steve took off the first week of December. He called Andy, his twenty-three-year-old son, and asked him to retrieve his freshmen term papers from the school.

The forced sabbatical promised to be Steve's opportunity to study and get ahead in his end-of-semester grading, but reading gave him a crushing headache and left him fatigued. Instead, he watched hours of Netflix. He was desperate to sleep, but in bed the familiar sensation of suffocation forced him to sit up, craving oxygen. He engineered several couch pillows into a makeshift hospital bed to prop himself in a relatively comfortable sitting position.

Steve had been fighting fatigue and a chronic cough throughout November. His boundless appetite had tapered to non-existent by Thanksgiving Day. Still, he hadn't visited the doctor until the following Thursday. Solid food still revolted him, in its place he sucked on green popsicles and occasionally forced down chicken noodle soup. By Wednesday evening he'd already seen more movies than he had in the previous three years.

After two days of antibiotics, Steve's condition declined, and he still had all of Thursday to endure before returning to Dr. Manchester on Friday morning. His back ached from sitting up two sleepless days and nights. The throbbing vein above his left temple tapped away at over 150 beats per minute.

Andy stopped by his father's solitary home on Thursday morning. Although he lived less than ten minutes away, he hadn't seen Steve in months. As soon as Andy entered the darkened living room, Steve ambushed him. "Where the hell have you been?" asked Steve.

Andy's guarded countenance transformed into one of astonishment and concern. Steve's face had taken on a grayish hue, his cheeks were sunken in, and his thinning brown hair was disheveled and oily. He shook from exhaustion. His average size frame typically weighed 190 pounds, but the illness had reduced him to less than 170.

"Have you been taking your medicine, Dad?" asked Andy.

"Of course. Did you bring my grading?"

"You look awful. We need to go back to your doctor."

"My papers? They would've been right in the middle of my desk. All you had to do is open your eyes."

"I didn't get a chance to stop by the school. You need to go back to the doctor."

"Damn it!" Steve said, coughing and wheezing. "You can't do me a simple favor?"

"Forget about your grading right now. Have you been taking your meds?"

"Yes! Of course I have. I already said that. They're worthless though."

"Are you feeling any better?"

"Look at me. What do you think? I feel like crap."

Andy placed his thumb on his father's trembling wrist. His pulse was racing. "Get dressed, Dad," said Andy. "You're going back to the doctor."

Dr. Manchester inspected the new x-ray with great concern. The grayscale photo displayed much larger white patches. "Unfortunately," said the doctor, "the pneumonia is unresponsive to oral antibiotics."

Steve was sent to Lofland Hospital for intravenous antibiotics. Andy checked Steve into the hospital and left him with the promise of returning on his way home from work. Nurses, techs, and others poked Steve and lobbed exasperating questions at him. He longed for the ability to lie down and sleep.

Instead of giving Steve antibiotics, a nurse administered a Lasix drip. The diuretic forced him to pee lakes and oceans, but relief began immediately. Within half an hour he was lying flat on his back. Sweet bliss. The

Lasix reduced Steve's weight by an additional fifteen pounds. He drifted off and slumbered soundly till the following afternoon.

Steve woke up rejuvenated. His clammy head was throbbing, but he could recline comfortably for the first time in a week. Although he wasn't lucid enough to study, the chicken fricassee smelled surprisingly appetizing.

That bastard, he thought. Why didn't Manchester send me to the ER in the first place? I oughta sue his ass. He texted Andy, making a second appeal to retrieve his grading. Andy didn't respond.

Steve came across a *Seinfeld* rerun and couldn't help but laugh along. Just as he began to relax, he heard the door subtly squeak as someone approached his bed. Steve assumed Andy had arrived, and was prepared to lecture him about his failure to reply to texts. Instead, a woman in a white lab coat sidled up to his bed.

"Hello, Mr. Dunham, I'm Dr. Smyth." She was a serious-mannered physician in her early fifties.

It's the best part of the episode, he thought. Can't she come back in five minutes? "Well, hello to you," he replied sarcastically.

She began to explain Steve's treatment. Already, he wanted her to stop talking. It was the Puffy Shirt episode, the best part was just ahead. He covertly adjusted his posture so Dr. Smyth wasn't blocking the television. Steve knew anything important being said would be explained again later, and if he were sent home he'd be given written instructions. Besides, he thought, where was this doctor a few days ago?

"We must discuss your condition," said Dr. Smyth. Steve's ears perked up, and he looked directly at her imposing scowl. "After looking at your x-ray and your blood work," she said, "and observing your accelerated heart rate, I've determined that you don't have pneumonia. Your heart is currently in a dangerous rhythm called atrial fibrillation. These symptoms have all been brought on because you're in the early stages of congestive heart failure."

What? Steve thought. What is she talking about? Heart failure? A blue baby flashed across his mind followed by a wheezing adolescent, too winded to keep up with his friends. "I haven't had problems with my heart in decades," he said.

"Your heart is tired and weak, causing fluid to accumulate around your heart. The fluid has filled your lungs. This is why you had such a hard time breathing." She explained that the Lasix removed the fluid from Steve's lungs, temporarily relieving the pressure on his chest. But his weakened heart was dying. He would need a transplant within three months. The doctor explained that he would need to see a congestive heart specialist and she left the room.

Steve sat in bewilderment as the cackling *Seinfeld* laugh track continued. The canned laughter served as a surreal juxtaposition, magnifying the gravity of the dumbfounding news.

Minutes earlier, Steve had been blissfully watching a sitcom, carefree and optimistic, but as the same episode hit its crescendo, dark violent clouds circled his mind and loomed over his future. The weight of the news pressed on him like a vice, more suffocating than the week of congestion he'd just endured. An infinite surplus of tomorrows had instantly been limited to ninety.

A life devoted to selfish pursuits sat squarely on Steve's shoulders. He longed for Andy's return, and the absence of his daughter, Becca, cut deeply. He hadn't talked to her in years. He refused to entertain thoughts of his ex-wife, Veronica. They were just too painful. Resisting the foreboding of his lonely room, Steve pretended a room of peace, and yet he couldn't block out the subtle din of hospital personnel, medical machinery, and the closing credits of *Seinfeld*.

Kevin Cobb

Chapter 2

Wayne Davidson's empty stomach protested when he pulled into the Walbrook parking lot. It was the Tuesday before Christmas and he had forgotten to grab a bite before heading to the retirement home. He entered the drab cafeteria to gather the volunteer service team, but no one was there. He left and headed down the green and white checkered linoleum hallway toward the event room.

A few minutes later a white van turned into the parking lot and found a spot in front of the long one-story building. Ranae Rhyner climbed out with five other SMU students. She held a white Chick-fil-a bag in one hand and pulled her blonde, windblown hair out of her eyes with the other. Although the dark afternoon was breezy, the temperature hovered above freezing.

The students walked through the dingy lobby and into the cafeteria, still pungent with the smell of beef stroganoff and canned corn. Ranae sat at a long table near the entrance while the rest of the service team proceeded to the back of the cafeteria.

Wayne returned to the cafeteria and noticed the petite blonde eating alone. His hunger emboldened him to sit across from her, disregarding his resolve to keep his distance. "Can I have one of those?" he asked.

Ranae glanced at her chicken nuggets with a look of confusion.

"I'm sorry," Wayne said, embarrassed. "Never mind. I'll eat later." He started to stand. "I apologize, I should—"

"No," she interrupted. "It's fine. Have as many as you want. It's not that, but, do you really want one? It's chicken, you know?"

"Yeah, I know."

"You can have the rest of them if you want. I don't mind. It's just, are you sure you want to give in? Just for chicken nuggets?"

Wayne looked at Ranae with equal confusion. "Well, yeah. I eat them all the time."

"What?" said Ranae, scrunching her forehead.

"Why is that weird?" asked Wayne.

"Well, it's chicken."

"Yeah, so?"

"Well, it's chicken, but it's still meat."

"So?"

"So aren't you a vegan?

Wayne laughed, waiting for the punch line. "A vegan?" he said. "Definitely not. No. Why did you think that?"

"Your bumper sticker."

"What bumper sticker?"

"The gold Honda is yours, isn't it?"

"Yeah."

"The front bumper sticker that says, 'I think, therefore I'm vegan.'"

13

Wayne sighed loudly and laughed. "That's my idiot roommate. He finds random bumper stickers and puts them on my car."

"That's too bad," said Ranae with a smirk. "Does that mean you don't have Bieber fever?"

"What?"

"Your rear bumper sticker says 'Bieber Fever,'" Ranae said, tilting her head flirtatiously.

"He thinks he's funny," said Wayne. "We've been roommates since college. Our freshman year I drove around with an Obama sticker on my front bumper and a Romney/Ryan on my rear bumper." Wayne snickered nervously. "Who knows how long it's been there. I once drove around for two years not knowing I had a sticker above my tailpipe that said 'I am a Jedi like my father before me'. It may explain why I haven't had a date in awhile."

"Nah," said Ranae, giggling and spontaneously placing her petite hand on Wayne's forearm. "I'm sure you have plenty of dates." She retracted her hand, but maintained penetrating eye contact.

Wayne turned his face to the side, unable to absorb the power of her radiant smile.

"I don't know," he said superfluously, unable to think. The shockwaves of Ranae's gentle touch reverberated through his arm, warming his body to the ends of his toes. He had done his best to hide his attraction to Ranae. Still, her infectious charisma, movie star smile, and mesmerizing blue eyes captivated him far more than he could disguise. She was a college senior, and he knew that he was no more than four years older than she, and yet as the leader of the service group, he wondered if his attraction to her was appropriate. In the five weeks Ranae had been volunteering at Walbrook Retirement Community, Wayne avoided speaking to her directly, and when he spoke to the group he resisted making eye contact with the five foot beauty.

Wayne couldn't remember why he had created the self-imposed restriction. He dared to look her in the face again and became hypnotized by her bewitching eyes. His resolve melted.

15

"Yeah," he said. "Those stickers make such a mess when you try to peel them off. So I just ignore them now. I haven't looked at my bumper in months. Thanks for the warning." He nervously plucked a chicken nugget from the rectangular box and shoved it into his mouth.

Ranae was enchanted by this lighter side of Wayne. She had been vaguely aware of the ulterior motive drawing her back to Walbrook. Her altruistic intentions were sincere, but it was the tall scruffy-faced seminary student that kept her coming back each week. Wayne was stoic and she was convinced he was too mature to notice a diminutive college girl. She hadn't ventured a conversation with him aside from short sentences, and always in reference to something related to their service at the retirement home. Watching him from across the table, however, she couldn't stop thinking about running her fingers through his thick brown hair.

"Actually," said Ranae. "There's *two* bumper stickers on the front of your car. They're both green. One is the vegan sticker, the other says, 'Go Green.'"

"Well, that's not so bad. I could probably stand being a bit greener."

"Couldn't we all. You should really get that—"

"Wayne," a loud voice interrupted from the back of the cafeteria. Lewis, the driver of the white van, entered the cafeteria. "Can you help me drive some of the residents tonight?" asked Lewis. "Brad, and Eddie want to go to Target, but I already told Anita, Donna, and Carolyn I would take them to the salon. Do you mind driving them?"

Wayne stood immediately, like he'd been caught doing something inappropriate. He walked toward the exit. "Sure," said Wayne. "No problem."

"Thanks," said Lewis. "I'll be back in an hour and a half or so to pick up the other students."

"Sounds great," said Wayne. "See you then."

Ranae stood to dispose of her trash.

Without stopping, Wayne looked back at Ranae. "You wanna hit up Target with three party animals?" he asked with a playful grin.

Ranae scurried to meet Wayne at the door. "Yeah, but only if I control the radio. No Bieber."

Chapter 3

Dr. Smyth transferred Steve to Our Lady of Angels Hospital in downtown Dallas. Cardiologist Johnathan Dekker placed him on several heart stabilizing medications. The hospital staff pulled fluid off his heart for the next three days until Steve's vitals stabilized. After a second evaluation, Dr. Dekker gave Steve's weakened heart the amended diagnosis of 2-4 years. Upon his discharge, Andy drove Steve to his home in Irving, Texas, a suburb immediately west of Dallas.

Despite Steve's improved prognosis, he understood the rarity of his heart condition and feared it may jeopardize his status as a transplant candidate. His lifelong pursuit of a doctoral degree had been rendered futile. *Why spend three of my four remaining good years completing something I'll never use?* he thought. *What's the point? The only reason to get a doctorate now is to have my title engraved on my gravestone.* At the age of forty-six Steve dropped out of graduate school for the last time.

As Christmas approached, Steve's anxiety elevated. He couldn't remember the last time he had looked forward to Christmas. He married Veronica at age eighteen upon her pregnancy with Rebecca; two years later Andy was born. Shortly after Andy's birth, Steve left Veronica. He spent every Christmas thereafter alone.

Andy dropped by for a brief visit three days before Christmas. His traditional Christmas gift to Steve was a bag of Berkley, blue-fleck Powerworms. As a preschooler, Andy hounded his mother to let him buy his estranged father a Christmas gift. Veronica asked Steve for a gift idea under five dollars. He gave her the exact name of his favorite fishing worms. Five-year-old Andy walked onto the porch with a bag of worms and a proud grin. Steve had never received a gift from Becca, so any gift from his youngest child was well received.

Eighteen years later, blue worms were still Andy's default Christmas gift. Steve played his part in the charade, embellishing excitement for another pack of worms. Steve came to view the gift as a passive aggressive symbol of Andy's disregard for a hollow childhood.

Steve handed Andy an envelope containing two gift certificates to Captain Fly's deep sea fishing charter. "Thanks, Dad," Andy said with a flat tone.

"Of course the second ticket is mine. You can't go fishing without taking your old man."

"Ashley doesn't like fishing anyway," Andy replied.

Father and son discussed the weather, the Texas Longhorns, and the Dallas Cowboys. Twenty minutes after arriving, Andy took his leave. His visit would be the highlight of Steve's Christmas season.

Steve mailed a Christmas card to Becca, and yet he knew he would receive no reply. On Christmas Eve he showered, shaved, and dressed. He tied his shoes and quickly stood up. As soon as he rose, his head was instantaneously flooded with darkness. He staggered in place until he found the sofa.

The dizzy spell passed, and he reminded himself to move slowly when standing. He shuffled out the door and into his white F-150. After settling into the driver's seat he took a few moments to catch his breath. How will I ever get back to school? he thought. I can't even walk to the damn truck; how am I going to teach? How am going to support myself? He started the truck and made his way to his favorite truck stop along Interstate 35-E.

The Maverick Star turned over its transient clientele practically every time he visited the sordid tavern, with the exception of six weathered truckers who regularly sat on the far left corner of the bar. The truckers were as loud and bawdy as Steve, but kept to their own. Steve had made attempts to chat with the truckers, but learned to keep clear. As long as Steve sat on the far right, most everyone he talked to were, as he preferred, out of town travelers. A man in a heavy winter coat walked through the front door and sat two stools from Steve at the bar. Steve discerned he was a northerner.

"Where ya from?" asked Steve, still catching his breath.

"Nebraska," answered the man. "Concordia, Nebraska."

Steve had never been to Nebraska. "Where ya heading?"

"Killeen. Killeen, Texas. I figure I still got about three hours."

"Nah," said Steve. "Not that long. Two and a half, tops. It's not that far and there's no traffic right now."

"Yeah?"

"Killeen. I've been there many times. Fort Hood is down there. We play Killeen Memorial every year in football. I coach high school football, a private school. It's a hell of a drive for a football game. Our district is damn near half the state. But they barely have enough kids for a team. It's usually not much of a game. I think last year we won by forty."

The man nodded politely as the bartender set a glass of Deep Eddy in front of him. He shifted his weight away from Steve and faced the television straight ahead.

"What are you doing in Killeen?" asked Steve.

"My daughter," said the man. "She moved down there in June to run an advertising firm. I haven't seen her since she left. I'm spending this next week with her." The man took a sip of his drink. "I meant to get down there yester—"

"My daughter, Becca, has a business degree. She graduated from Oklahoma State two years ago and she's already got a job at a big insurance company. This year she'll make sixty thousand dollars. She's only twenty-four. Can you believe that? Sixty grand." The annoyed traveler nodded and stared at his drink, then away from Steve into the kitchen. After a few minutes of silence Steve turned to the man. "Well," said Steve, "the weather should be a lot better for you in Killeen than Nebraska this week, huh? It might be in the Seventies and Eighties on Friday."

"I hope so. I brought my clubs."

"You'll find some great courses down in Killeen."

"Yeah?"

"I'm sure of it. Killeen is on the edge of hill country."

"Yeah, Stacy loves it down there. I hope to check it out."

"I went down there with my second wife to a bed and breakfast. We inner-tubed down the Brazos, and I lost a twenty dollar pair of sun glasses. It was just us and another couple. They were the only other guests there. It was awkward at first. Every time we soaked in the hot tub they were there. But the woman was a prostitute. He brought a hooker to a bed and breakfast!" Steve laughed, amused by his own story. "When he was taking a phone call I asked her what her rate was. A grand for the whole weekend."

The man responded with a token laugh. Over the man's shoulder, Steve noticed a blonde female sitting five stools to the left. He was content with an evening of male banter, and yet the potential of female companionship for the night was far preferable.

"Have a safe trip, buddy," Steve said, standing up.

As Steve stood he was quickly revisited by a partial blackout. He steadied himself, walked to the far side of the middle-aged woman, and sat beside her with a thud,

25

relieved to be seated again. He opened his mouth to speak, but realized he still hadn't caught his breath. He studied her out of his peripheral vision as he waited for his breathing to subside. She was in her late thirties, dark black roots pushed up faded blonde hair, and her face was much harder than he had previously thought. She wore a light pink jacket. Steve failed to notice her demeanor had stiffened upon his arrival, and she had turned away from him.

"Where ya from?" asked Steve.

The wary stranger opened the trifold menu and stared at it in deep consideration.

Speaking louder, he tried again. "Where ya heading to?"

"Nowhere really," she answered curtly.

"I mean, are you traveling?

"I'm meeting a friend."

"Where are you from?"

"I'm just meeting a friend."

"Do you live here in Irving? I'm a teacher here. And a football coach."

"Yeah?" she said, a spark of curiosity in her voice. "My nephew plays football at MacArthur."

"I coach at Alexandria"

"Oh," she said, interest waning.

"It's a private school."

The lady returned her attention to the menu.

"What position does your nephew play?" asked Steve.

"Uh, let's see. I don't remember."

"Offense or defense?"

"Well, he doesn't get to touch the ball much, I know that."

"Defense maybe?"

"He's number Nighty-Two. I know that."

27

"Ah, a lineman. I bet he's a good sized boy to play on the line at MacArthur."

Her eye's brightened, and she swiveled her stool to face Steve. "Yeah, when my sister had him he weighed fourteen pounds. He was the heaviest baby born in Dallas County that month. Little Big Tank. That was his nickname. Now we just call him Tank. He's so strong, but he's a sweetheart."

"Ty 'Tank' Walker? Tank Walker's your nephew?"

She smiled big and laughed. "Yes, that's him. You've heard of him?"

Steve recognized a familiar spark in her eyes. Typically, when he saw this twinkle he would push things to the next level by introducing himself and asking the conquest her name. He believed he had an uncanny knack for capturing a lady's interest with simple conversation. Some told him his sparkling green eyes held his allure, others told him it was his piercing wit. He didn't know what caused it; he only knew that it existed and that this bleach blonde had bought in. Not every woman was ensnared by his enigmatic charm, but he recognized the ones who did right away.

Tonight was no good, however; he knew it. He still hadn't caught his breath from the journey from one stool to the other. He had dropped so much weight, yet he never felt heavier. What the hell am I doing? he thought. Where am I going with this? I can't walk across the bar without an oxygen tank. How am I going to take her home?

Steve stood and the dark fogginess returned. "Oh yeah," said Steve, steadying himself by grabbing the bar. "Everyone's heard of Tank Walker. No doubt he'll be playing in Austin after he graduates." Steve looked deeply into her eyes. "Have a pleasant time with your friend." Walking to the door, he passed a man entering the truck stop in a baseball cap and denim jacket. Steve turned and watched him walk to the bar and sit on the very stool he had just vacated. The man gave the blonde woman a kiss.

"Hm." Steve mumbled to himself. "Who the hell do I think I am?"

Kevin Cobb

He drove home and opened a bottle of Cruzan. Although he had always enjoyed the peace and freedom that accompanied single life, the shifting status of his health tinted his outlook. The silence was palpable, the loneliness terrifying. He filled his cup half full of Coke and topped it off with the Virgin Islands' rum.

On Christmas Day, Steve placed a rum-filled flask in his inside coat pocket and drove to AMC 30. He evenly dispersed the rum throughout four Cokes while watching two movie premiers. Afterwards, he schlepped home and passed out in the recliner while watching *Die Hard II*.

Teachers were due back to Alexandria for the Spring Semester on January 3rd. His gait was slow, and he couldn't walk far without a respite, but on Christmas day he strode onto the sidewalk and began his quest to get back into shape. Every fifty yards or so, he paused and stood in place to catch his breath until he eventually circled the block.

The next day Steve returned to the heart clinic complaining he didn't have the strength to return to work. Dr. Dekker adjusted his blood pressure meds and assured him that he would soon see a significant improvement. The following day he walked around the block without stopping. Three days later he trekked two effortless miles. By the end of the week, he added sit-ups and push-ups and took three long walks a day.

On New Year's Eve, he looked at himself in the mirror. He no longer saw a withering heart patient, too weak to walk to his truck without a break. Instead, he saw a trim, healthy man ready for several years of productive living. He weighed the same as he had when he married Veronica, and he felt healthier than any time he could remember. His strength increased daily, and he began to wonder if Dr. Dekker's estimate of four years was conservative. He walked away from the mirror hopeful that his heart would last another decade.

Kevin Cobb

2017

Chapter 4

The hot pink ball rolled down the middle of the lane before it drifted off to the right and into the gutter.

"Almost," said Kurt Hitzges. "You nearly got some pins that time."

"Can I go to the arcade now?" asked Monica.

"No," said Kurt. "We're bowling. That's why you came with us. You begged to come with us."

"Mom gave me money for the arcade."

"Let her go," said Julie, laughing. "What does it matter?"

"Why don't you let me turn the bumpers on?" asked Kurt. "It'll be a lot more fun for you."

"No," said Monica. "That's for babies."

"Yeah," said Julie. "Be patient, Kurt." Julie turned to Monica. "Don't listen to him. Keep aiming for that middle arrow and keep your arm straight. You'll be fine."

"It's the same as Wii bowling, Mon," said Kurt. "Just do the same thing."

The ball rose out of the rattling ball return, and Monica picked it up with both hands. She shuffled toward the narrow lane and dropped the ball. It rolled slowly down the middle of the lane and drifted into the right gutter.

"Almost, Mon," said Julie. She stood and fished a ball out of the ball return. "Just a little harder next time."

"Did you get back yesterday?" asked Kurt.

"I wish. No. We got home the night before. Dad always makes us get up first thing on New Year's Day to drive the whole way. We got in that night." Julie lined up and threw the ball down the lane, knocking over six pens.

"Did you visit Florida State?" asked Kurt.

"Yes! It was the best part of the trip. Besides the beach it was the *only* good part. I can't wait to go. It's gorgeous. I love the dorms. I'll get my own bathroom! And the beach is, like, forty-five minutes away."

Julie lined up and threw her ball down the lane, knocking over two of the remaining four pins.

"Can you believe we're graduating in five months?" asked Kurt.

"No," said Julie. "It seems like we were just freshmen." She sat next to Kurt as he stood.

"Not to me," said Kurt. "Every school year seemed like a lifetime, until this year. This year is flying."

"What about you? Did you get accepted into UTD?"

"Not yet, but I'm going to get my application in this week."

"You haven't applied yet? Hitz, you got to get on this. You're running out of time. Get it in right away. Get it in today."

Kurt threw a heavy blue ball and knocked over nine pins. The last pin wobbled, but didn't fall.

"Crap!" said Kurt. "I thought I had it. One of us needs to get a strike."

"We haven't even gotten a spare."

"Not yet."

"Seriously, Hitz. You're running out of time. You need to get your application in now."

"Yeah, I know. I'll get it done tonight. In the mail tomorrow."

"Can I go to the arcade now?" asked Monica.

"We're six frames in," said Kurt. "We've only got four to go."

Monica sighed dramatically and sat down. She put her face in her hands and let out another dramatic sigh.

"Awe, come on," said Julie. "Let her go. She just wants to go to the arcade."

Monica peeked at Kurt for a response. Kurt put his heels together and looked intently down the lane. "No," he said. "I can't see her from here. Mom would kill me if I let her go alone, and we came here to bowl. Watch me pick up this spare." Kurt's ball moved quickly down the lane, missing the pin to the left.

"Damn it," said Kurt.

"Can I go to the arcade now?" asked Monica.

"It's your turn, Mon," said Julie. "Give it another try."

Monica stood next to the ball return with her shoulders slumped. She reached down and grabbed her ball.

"Okay, Mon," said Kurt. "You're good at aiming for the arrows. You just need to give it some power. Throw that thing hard. Really let it go and you'll get some pins."

"Let's go, Monica!" said Julie, clapping enthusiastically. "You got this!"

Monica clutched the ball with one hand and scooted toward the lane. When she swung the ball forward, it flung out of her hand, bounced off the middle of the adjacent lane to the right, and landed two lanes over in the far gutter.

Julie muffled a startled laugh, and Kurt stood in stunned silence. Monica slowly turned around like a dog caught eating from the trash can, smiling sheepishly. Kurt looked around, but there were no bowlers within eight lanes. No one had noticed. Julie let out an unrestrained laugh. Monica shrugged and grinned.

"Okay. You win," said Kurt. "Let's go to the arcade."

Chapter 5

On the first Monday of the year, Steve arrived early for teacher in-service, a morning full of staff meetings and an afternoon in his classroom preparing for the upcoming semester.

At noon the administration provided a catered lunch for the faculty and staff. He sat at a center table among his colleagues. Although his strength had improved significantly, a marked change in Steve's countenance was evident to the Alexandria faculty. The red faced coach was a pale, shriveled shell of himself, and with the uncertainty of his future health, the faculty was unsure how to greet him.

The older female teachers broke the ice by doting on him. Other teachers joined in, and eventually each teacher spoke to Steve, offering encouraging words about his weight loss or his speedy recovery. Almost every teacher told Steve they were praying for him and used the phrase "you look great."

Unsolicited, Steve told the story of his false pneumonia. His colleagues offered feigned interest, mechanical platitudes, and disingenuous smiles. Always cheerful and eager to reward a joke with laughter, Lisa Dwyer mirrored his story with cackling. The positive feedback intoxicated Steve, prompting him to press on. His voice rose louder, and he added hand gestures and dramatic pauses.

He concluded his monologue, then stood to fill a second plate. A female teacher handed him a loose piece of paper. "Pick three slots and pass it on," she said. He took the lunch duty roster from her, pulled a pen from his pocket, and looked around for a hard surface.

"Hey, Lisa," said Steve with a smirk. "Come over here. I need something flat to write on."

The joke silenced the room, and the false energy, which had been graciously provided for Steve's sake, dissipated. "Oh, come on," said Steve. "Why does everybody have to be so serious?" The room was unnervingly still. Lisa contrived a failed smile, her face flushed.

Steve returned to the catering table to refill his plate with chips and brisket queso. Tom Sturm, the head football coach, approached Steve. "What the hell was that?" said Tom. "Are you trying to get fired?"

"Oh, relax," replied Steve, waving an apathetic hand at Tom. "It was just a joke. She knows that."

"No man, you don't *say* things like that. Say something like that in class and see what happens. You'll be lucky if Lisa doesn't sue you."

With a revitalized appetite, Steve shrugged off Tom and loaded more fajita meat onto his plate.

The next morning, Steve entered Alexandria with a spring in his step. The students were returning, and normalcy would soon follow. Fifteen minutes before class began, Alexandria's front doors were unlocked and students trickled into the building.

A few minutes later a blond boy stuck his head in the door. "Coach Dunham!" he yelled. The student disappeared and returned seconds later with several other cheerful students. Over the next ten minutes, three dozen teenagers circulated in and out of his room. Many conversed from a distance about his eerie physical transformation, while others rushed Steve's desk with salutations. Class was due to start momentarily. Steve's first period students took their seats, while two dozen others lingered. "Time for class," said Steve firmly and loudly. "I'm not writing y'all tardy slips. If you're not in my first period class, get out," he said with a wry smile. "You'll be sick of seeing me soon enough," he said. "Go to class."

Steve's first period class settled in. He shut the door and returned to his desk, basking in the glow of being missed. He fully understood that teaching was the one thing in life he did well. He was back where he belonged.

Steve's return to the classroom affirmed that his life hadn't ceased, but the weekends were less inspiring. Whether at home or at the Maverick Star, his time off was primarily spent drinking or exercising. He escorted female company home just once before realizing he was physically limited to conversation. To keep himself occupied, he bought a stationary bike and rode five days a week.

In March he retrieved his mountain bike from the garage and rode the residential streets of his neighborhood. He attempted to jog, but failed to make it a half mile before getting winded. Since returning to school, Steve had gained ten pounds and resembled a healthy version of his previous self. After this healthy weight gain, he was still twenty pounds lighter than before the hospitalization. This unfamiliar nimbleness gave Steve the illusion of energy and the false assumption that his heart was healing.

In addition to assisting Coach Sturm each autumn with the football team, Steve led the baseball team each spring. As soon as the school year ended, he dug his boat out of storage and began fishing two to three days a week.

Ten days before the beginning of the new school year, Steve was enjoying a productive day of fishing on Lake Lewisville. The wind had picked up, however, and the south side of the bridge become choppy, moving to the southwest like a large river. The fish finder informed Steve he had drifted to the peripheral of the school of hybrid striped bass he had chased all day. He started the motor and centered the boat. Over the next half an hour he caught three more hybrids, repositioning his boat after each fish. Fatigue subtly set in, and his body became sluggish.

Steve hooked into another and began to reel it in. This one pulled harder than any he had caught. He reeled it, sensing the fish's life struggle on every crank of the reel. When he brought the fish aboard, he was disappointed to see it was only a twelve inch sand bass. He turned to reposition the boat, but had to catch his breath first. The next fish fought tougher yet. After five minutes of reeling, the fish was winning the battle.

He wanted to curl up and take a nap, but he still had to make his way to shore and pull the boat from the water. He opened his pocket knife and cut the line, freeing the ensnared fish. His body ached, as though he had the flu.

With great effort, Steve navigated the boat out of the angling tumult to the boat launch, beaching it to the left of the ramp. The uphill walk to his truck forced him to rest before he backed the trailer into the water. He sat in the truck taking deep breaths, attempting to regain the strength to crank the boat onto the trailer. The longing to sleep returned, and he considered lying across the cab, but another truck and trailer pulled into the lot, ready to launch.

By the time he cranked the boat onto the trailer he could barely stand. He drove thirty yards into the parking lot and stopped to strap the boat down. He closed his eyes and focused on his breathing.

As Steve waited for his breathing to stabilize, he grabbed his phone and googled "organ transplant". The first page he visited reported that 120,000 Americans currently waited for an organ. Narrowing his search to "heart transplant", he stumbled upon the Our Lady of Angels Hospital web site. American hospitals perform approximately 3,300 heart transplants per year. OLA accounted for about sixty a year. Transplanted hearts typically came from donors ages 18-30, from all races and genders.

Kevin Cobb

Steve set his phone on the passenger seat and took a long deep breath before exiting the truck. Five minutes later he returned to the driver seat, panting and gasping. He knew the end had begun, and he wondered if his heart would make it to Christmas.

Chapter 6

John Paul spun the tires of his Toyota Corolla as soon as the light turned green, speeding ahead of the Mustang in the adjacent lane. The driver of the Mustang ignored the mystic teal sedan. John Paul loudly wound out each of the first four gears of the manual transmission before decelerating to the speed limit of forty.

"Why would you want to run a marathon?" asked John Paul, glancing at his phone.

"I don't know," replied Kurt from the back seat. "I haven't done anything since basketball season."

"Why don't you just join a gym, Hitz?" said Elio in the passenger seat, eyes glued to his own phone. "Or maybe a poetry class or something,"

"I've got to find something. I'm bored. I need something to do till I go to college."

"Zumba?" said John Paul. "Pilates? Maybe you could *do* a Milf?"

"No. I'm serious. I haven't done anything since we graduated. I've always wanted to run a marathon. If we don't do it now we never will."

"So what?" said Elio.

"Yeah, who cares?" said John Paul, one hand on the steering wheel, the other replying to a text. "I'm fine going my whole life without running a marathon."

"Dude," said Kurt, looking over John Paul's shoulder. "Quit texting."

Three years earlier Kurt's father died in a head-on collision with a texting driver.

John Paul set his phone on the column. The decaying family car moved past the town square and north toward Studebaker's cafe.

Kurt stared blankly out the left rear passenger window in disbelief. It was nearly the middle of August, and he was still in Rockwall, Texas, a suburb twenty minutes east of Dallas. He had received an acceptance letter to the University of Texas at Dallas, but had no money for school and he had failed to secure grants and loans to pay for the first year.

After his father's death, Kurt's mother was left to run the cattle ranch alone. She soon fell into debt and was forced to sell their 1,200 acre property. The new owner allowed her to pay rent to stay in the ranch house. Preoccupied with hardship, Mrs. Hitzges neglected Kurt's college education, leaving him to his own devices. He was aware of student grants and loans, but knew nothing about due dates. By the time he pursued financial aid, it was too late. Instead of fall classes he would be working on the assembly line at Maples Industries with the hope of attending the following year.

The three boys had attended school together since the third grade. When they began playing basketball in junior high, they developed a bond that would become a lifelong friendship. The boys were so inseparably associated with one another the basketball team referred to the three as 'the Arabs'. Kurt had curly jet black hair and a dark complexion, but his ancestors came from Poland and Italy.

"I haven't run since basketball ended," said Elio, still looking at his phone. "I don't miss it either."

49

"Yeah," said John Paul. "Why do you have to drag us into it?"

"I'm going to do it either way, but I'd rather not run alone."

"Why don't you ask Julie?" asked John Paul.

"She won't be back from Florida State yet," said Kurt.

"Lucky her," said John Paul.

"I'm down," Elio said, putting his phone into his pocket. "I'll run with you, Hitz. What else have I got to do?"

"Bullshit," said John Paul. "You'll back out. When is it?"

"December 16th," said Kurt.

"December?" said Elio. "Why are you worried about it now? That's four months from now."

"You can't just show up and run a marathon," said Kurt. "You have to train for it."

"I'm not running every day for four months. Get back with me in November."

"I told you he'd back out," said John Paul.

"I'm not backing out. If he wants to run, I'm down. I just don't want to spend half the year running. What a beating."

"Nah, you'll back out," said John Paul. "I'll bet ya a hundred dollars."

"You're on," said Elio, extending his hand to John Paul. "I'm running."

"Nah, now you'll run just to get the money."

"Fine, make it twenty. Twenty won't make a difference whether I run or not."

"Fine," replied John Paul as he shook Elio's hand.

As they passed Kroger an eighteen-wheel truck crept along the left lane. John Paul was about to pass the truck to the right when it abruptly cut him off to turn into the parking lot. John Paul slammed on his brakes to prevent a collision.

"What a douche!" John Paul yelled, simultaneously braking and honking his horn. He sped around the truck without taking his hand off the horn, pulling directly in front of the truck and braking hard. The Corolla came to a complete stop, forcing the truck to brake abruptly.

"What the hell are you doing?" yelled Elio.

"Me?" replied John Paul. "Did you see what that asshole did?"

The boys heard a siren from behind the truck. Before they knew it a police cruiser pulled along the car and motioned for John Paul to pull into the parking lot.

"Is he pointing at *me*?" yelled John Paul. "Seriously? He needs to get *that* douche!" John Paul pointed to the truck driver.

"Just pull over," said Kurt.

John Paul pulled into the parking lot screaming obscenities. The truck turned in as well, driving past John Paul's car and on toward the store.

The officer stepped out of his cruiser and approached John Paul's window.

"What did ya pull me over for?" yelled John Paul. "Get that shit head! Didn't you see what he did to me? Nearly killed us. This ain't even the truck entrance. If I hadn't pounded the hell out of my brakes—"

"Calm down, son," said the officer. "I'm not giving you a ticket. Not yet anyway. But someone needs to put some sense into you."

"Me? That guy is driving like—"

"Son," the officer interrupted forcefully. "Stop talking before I change my mind. You need to understand something. You don't want to mess with a truck like that. Whether you're in the right or wrong, it doesn't matter. If you take on a forty ton truck you're going to lose. A truck that big needs a whole lot of space to stop. You're lucky he didn't flatten you. Got it?"

John Paul calmed down, but said nothing.

"You got it?" the officer repeated.

John Paul nodded.

"May I see your license and proof of insurance?"

John Paul let out an inconvenienced sigh, pulled his license and insurance card from his wallet, and handed it to the officer without looking at him.

The officer looked at the license closely and scanned the car's interior, making eye contact with Kurt, then Elio. "Where you boys heading?"

"Just driving around," said John Paul.

"Okay," the officer said, as he returned John Paul's license. "You boys drive carefully and stay out of the way of those trucks. And have a pleasant evening." He tipped his hat and returned to his cruiser.

"What a douche," said John Paul.

"How come you're pissed at him?" asked Elio. "He let you off."

"Let me off? I didn't do anything. He let that truck go and harassed me because I'm Arab."

"How could he tell you were Arab from behind?" said Kurt.

"You're lucky he didn't give you a ticket," Elio added.

"A ticket for what?" said John Paul. "Saving us from getting killed by that shithead? I didn't break any laws."

"I don't know," said Kurt. "You must've done something wrong; you nearly got us killed."

Kevin Cobb

Chapter 7

Ranae's alarm clock beeped at 4:25 a.m. Wayne rolled over and glared at her. She didn't move.

"Rabbit, that's yours," said Wayne.

Ranae didn't respond. After several more seconds he reached over Ranae and switched her alarm off.

"Time to get up, Rabbit," said Wayne.

Ranae rolled from her side to her back with a look of defiance, eyes still closed. "Do I have to?"

"No. Just stay home and eat breakfast with me. You don't need this job anyway. Just stay home and study."

"I wish," Ranae said, sitting up in bed. "It's fine. I'll be back by noon."

"We don't need this job. Just go back to sleep. In a month or so you'll be a nurse. "

"No. We aren't jumping into debt two weeks after our wedding. Anyway, I like the lady who hired me. I loved working at the bakery back home. It'll be fine."

"It's only for a month or so. There's no debt."

Ranae ran her hand down Wayne's chest, grazing his skin with her fingertips. "Love you, babe," she said. She kissed him on the forehead and stepped out of bed, stretched, and ambled toward the shower.

Samson's Grocery was three blocks from their apartment in Lakewood, a neighborhood in northeast Dallas. Ranae parked in the empty parking lot near the main entrance at 4:55. She sat in her car staring intently at the store's front door. She contemplated whether she should wait five minutes until her shift started or go ahead and get it over with? Wayne was right, she thought. *I don't need this job. If I'm not working I can pass my boards sooner.*

She closed her eyes and thought about the first day of the honeymoon. She had allowed herself to believe the nine day vacation was endless, but less than two weeks later she sat alone in a Samson's parking lot before dawn. She usually began each morning with a jog, but it seemed uncivilized to rise in the middle of the night to run before a job she didn't want. Despite her fresh memories of dulcet lapping waves and hypnotic seagulls, the honeymoon was clearly over.

Ranae took a deep breath and exhaled slowly. She snatched her hat off the passenger seat and stepped out of the car. When she reached the store entrance, the front door was locked. The store didn't open till 5:30, but she had been instructed to clock in at 5:00.

She had spent the previous day at the store watching safety videos and filling out paperwork, but that was in the middle of the day. No one told her the door would be locked, and she wasn't given a passcode. Ranae pushed her forehead against the glass door to peek into the storefront. The building was fully lit, and she could see store employees preparing to open. She knocked on the door, then glanced nervously at her phone for the time. No one came to her aid.

Two minutes after five she caught the attention of a lady in a red Samson's vest standing by a cash register. With a frown of annoyance, the woman shook her head and pointed to her watch. Ranae continued pounding until she dawdled to the door. "We don't open till 5:30," said the woman.

"I work here," Ranae responded, pointing to her tall baker's hat.

The employee opened the door. "You're supposed to come in through the back door. Before 5:30 you have to come in the back door."

"I'm sorry," said Ranae, entering the store. "It's my first day."

The bothered employee responded with a blank nod and returned to the cash register. Ranae sprinted to the back of the store. The bakery paralleled the produce aisle against the far right wall. She put her hat on and cautiously stepped beyond the counter and into the back room. A middle aged woman placed large sheet trays of dough into a tall metal cabinet on wheels. She wore the same outfit as Ranae except that she wore a dusty brown-stained apron over her bakery uniform. The lady turned. "You're late," she said. "It's 5:04. I'm pretty lenient for the most part, but one thing I don't tolerate is tardiness."

"I'm sorry, Leslie. It won't happen again."

"Besides, you're supposed to come in through the back door before 5:30."

"Yes, ma'am. I'm sorry. It won't happen again."

"Grab an apron," said Leslie, pointing to the lowest drawer of a prep island. "I need you to take over here," said Leslie. "I need to get the front ready to open."

Ranae tied on an apron and washed her hands. "Okay," she said. "What can I do for you?"

Leslie grabbed a box from a flat cart next to the rolling cabinet and threw it onto the counter. "Put the rest of these cinnamon rolls on sheet trays till you have six trays. Then put them into the rotary," she said, pointing to a large dingy oven. "Have you ever used a rotary oven?"

"Yes, ma'am, I have."

Kevin Cobb

"Get them into the oven in the next ten minutes." Leslie shuffled to the front of the bakery.

Ranae looked down at a sheet tray half filled with frozen knots of dough. She read the box Leslie had placed on the counter:

Frozen Homemade Cinnamon Rolls

Ranae smirked. A grocery store bakery shared little similarity with the bakery she had worked in back home.

The summer after high school, Ranae worked at Stockslager's Bakery in Union, Ohio. Luann Stockslager, a German Baptist grandmother, owned the bakery and insisted everything be made with fresh ingredients from scratch. Ranae arrived at Stockslager's each morning at 2:00 a.m. When she arrived, the dough had already been made and proofed. First she kneaded the dough to push out the air pockets, then rolled it into a flat rectangle and brushed the rolled dough liberally with butter. The rectangle was saturated with cinnamon and brown sugar before she rolled it into a large log and cut it into two dozen cinnamon rolls. After they were baked and glazed, the rolls attracted customers from all over the Miami Valley. The process created the most heavenly aroma she could imagine. At this Dallas area grocery chain, however, she only needed to transfer the rolls from a box to a tray, put them into the oven, and frost them as they came out.

Ranae finished traying the last of the frozen cinnamon rolls and began loading them into the cabinet. A short chubby man in his early twenties lumbered into the room. He wore a Samson's bakery uniform and hastily put on an apron. As he reached behind to tie his apron strings he glared at Ranae with a cross face. "I do the cinnamon rolls," he said. He walked to Ranae's counter, stepped in front of her, and finished loading the last pan.

"Leslie asked me to do the cinnamon rolls," she said.

"Uh-uh. I always do the cinnamon rolls. Find somethin' else to do." He pulled the cabinet of rolls toward the rotary oven.

Ranae was confused, unsure what to do with her hands. "What should I do then?" she asked.

"Tray up the French bread. It's in the walk-in."

Ranae obediently walked toward the walk-in freezer. "I'm Ranae," she said affably.

The man paused long enough to ogle her. The bakery uniform and cap couldn't veil her inherent magnetism. He gave her a lewd stare and a suspicious smile. "Hey," he said, attempting to make deep eye contact. "Welcome to Samson's. I'm Rodney."

Before she could respond to his creepy greeting, Leslie reentered the room. "Rodney!" yelled Leslie. "I'm not going to tolerate you being late! It's 5:25. We open in five minutes. You haven't been on time all week!"

"Calm down," said Rodney. "I'm here, ain't I?"

Ranae walked into the cooler and let the door shut behind her. The crisp air provided a welcome break from the stuffy bakery. She put her hands on her forehead and massaged her sleep-deprived head. Her moment of peace was broken by the escalating exchange between Leslie and Rodney. Ranae looked at the flat cart in front of her and shook her head. The cart was loaded with several boxes marked:

Gourmet French Bread

One thought occurred to Ranae; start studying tonight.

Kevin Cobb

Chapter 8

After Ranae left for Samson's, Wayne showered, dressed, and headed downtown to Bailiff Industrial Supply. He unlocked the front door and walked through the storefront, past the counter and into the office to clock in before 7:00. The air-conditioned office beckoned him to stay, but he resisted, exiting into the warehouse, smoldering from a week of triple digit temperatures. After turning on all the lights in the building, he walked to the dock and opened one of the four large dock doors, revealing a large swath of the Dallas skyline. The gaping door brought no relief. It would be another scorcher.

Wayne opened the other three dock doors. An open trailer obstructed the view of the third door. The large box truck had backed up to the dock overnight. Wayne engaged the dock leveler and lowered the end onto the back of the truck connecting it to the dock. He jumped off the dock and into the parking lot to chock the tires.

As soon as he jumped down, the sweet aroma of an uptown bakery distinguished itself among the exhaust fumes and blistering asphalt. He wondered how Ranae's first day at Samson's was going. Did she stick it out or was she already home studying? He pushed the rubber block in front of the right rear tire and climbed back into the warehouse.

He pushed the pallet jack into the truck and started unloading the pallets. Each pallet held a large cardboard box full of industrial supplies such as electric motors, generators, fans, and tools. The pallets stood double stacked in the trailer. Wayne could use the forklift, but he preferred the pallet jack.

The truck driver climbed the cement steps and entered the unlocked warehouse door. "Hey, he's back!" said the driver.

"What's up, bud?" Wayne said, pulling another pallet from the truck. "How've you been, Gordon?"

"Can't complain," said Gordon. "So, yer married, huh?"

"Yep," said Wayne, raising his left hand to display his new wedding band. "We just got back Sunday. My sunburn is still itching like mad."

"Oh, yeah. You're strapped to the ball and chain now," Gordon said, laughing at his own joke.

"Chain me up. I'm ready." Wayne reentered the truck and retrieved another pallet. Gordon moved to the edge of the dock to peek into the truck.

"I was married for thirteen years," said Gordon. "Lucky thirteen, I always say. I barely remember my wedding. But my divorce was the best day of my life."

Wayne pulled the next double stacked pallet from the truck without looking at Gordon.

"Don't worry," Gordon continued. "After a decade or so she might let you out early for good behavior."

Wayne dropped the pallet in line with the rest and dragged the pallet jack back into the truck.

"Of course, you got a real pretty wife," said Gordon. "One that won't bark at you all the time, I bet."

"Yeah, Ranae's great. I married way out of my league." Wayne took a step back and surveyed the remaining freight. The top pallet of a double stack had shifted and the large cardboard box precariously leaned to the left. The load could collapse if he attempted to remove it with the jack. He needed the forklift. Shaking his head, Wayne stepped on the forklift and drove it around to square it with the open truck door. He hated to unload trucks with the forklift.

When Wayne began working at Bailiff, he took a three day forklift certification course. The graphic safety videos and unsettling safety statistics kept him in a constant state of paranoia. Each time he stepped on the forklift his mind wondered to the countless forklift accidents uploaded to YouTube.

Wayne mounted the battery-powered forklift and entered the trailer, squaring the forklift with the bottom pallet. He raised the forks and reached under the top pallet. He tilted the forks and lifted them slightly before retracting the load. Wayne backed the forklift out of the truck and placed the undamaged pallet in line with the others.

As soon as Gordon left, Wayne began entering the bulk items into inventory. He dreaded this task because bulk items required a forklift or an order picker. After a two week break from Bailiff, his warehouse anxieties were renewed. He scanned the barcode on a large generator with his handheld scanner and drove toward its assigned location. After putting up a two hundred pound electric motor, Wayne stepped off the forklift and onto the order picker.

Wayne scooped up a pallet of several large boxes on the rear of the order picker. The forklift was not as intimidating to Wayne as the picker. The forklift stayed on the ground while the picker raised the entire cab, operator and all, to the height necessary to manually place items in their respective locations. The picker could raise the operator up to thirty feet in the air.

Wayne drove the picker to aisle 2340 and lifted himself to the fourth level, twenty-five feet in the air. He haltingly slid a hundred pound box onto the top shelf. The cab swayed as the weight of the box transferred onto the shelf, and Wayne tightened in fear. This is it, he thought.

Kevin Cobb

Heaven? Hell? Reincarnation? Oblivion? I'm about to find out the truth of the afterlife. Millions and millions of people have died, and every one of them know more about the afterlife then I do. The only reason I believe the Bible is because my mom did. What would I believe if Mom had been an atheist? What if I had been born in India? He lowered the cab and proceeded to the next location.

Soon after Wayne entered the last of the large items, a fellow employee, emerged from the office and began loading the small items onto a metal cart.

"Wayne!" The employee shouted with glee. "You're back. I was beginning to wonder if you'd ever come back."

Wayne unhooked his harness, stepped off the picker, and shook his hand. "Hey, Junior," said Wayne. "What's new around here?"

"Nothing," said Junior. "It's just hot. Smelly and hot. Are y'all staying at your apartment or did you get a new place?"

"No. Still in my apartment. Let me get this air conditioner up and I'll help you." Wayne stepped onto the picker, loaded the large box, and drove into the center of the warehouse. He returned the empty picker to the dock, took off the harness, and stepped off. A familiar sense of calm flooded his countenance, the relief of knowing he wouldn't die in the warehouse today.

Ranae sat at the kitchen table when Wayne arrived home. Her laptop was open, and she was writing in a thick paperback book. She rushed to the door and met him with a long hug and a loving kiss.

"How's the new job?" asked Wayne.

Ranae looked up with a pouty frown and sad eyes. "Don't make me go back there," she said.

"That bad, huh?"

"I've been studying for my boards since I got home. I've got to get out of there. It's not even a real bakery. We don't actually bake anything. We just reheat rolls and put boxed bread into individual bags so customers think they're fresh."

"What did you expect? It's a grocery store bakery. It's not your Amish bakery."

"German Baptist," she corrected.

"I know," said Wayne with a wink.

"It's not just the bakery. It's the people. They're all miserable."

Wayne walked into the kitchen and opened the refrigerator. "So did you quit?" he asked.

Ranae walked after him. "No. I'm just being a baby. It'll be fine. Tomorrow will be better."

Wayne closed the refrigerator door, opened a cabinet, and pulled out a protein bar.

"Don't eat too much," said Ranae. "I'll make us something soon."

"Not for me, Rabbit. I've got Walbrook tonight."

"Tonight? We've only been back two days."

"It's Thursday. Sorry. I haven't been there in three weeks. Plus, the students come back today. I can't miss their first day back."

"Really? Already?"

"Well, the returning students anyway. Most are already back in town and want to start this week. I couldn't tell them no."

"No, I guess not," Ranae said. "Can I still go with you, even though I've graduated? I miss Walbrook."

"Of course, you're always welcome. But not tonight. You need to study. I won't be happy till you're happy. So study." Wayne smiled and gave her another kiss. "I'll be back soon. Love you." he opened the front door and looked back with a smile.

"Love you, too, babe," she said, watching Wayne descend the stairwell.

Wayne arrived at Walbrook fifteen minutes before the service started. The service team visited Walbrook twice a week. On Tuesday evenings the service team spent time with the residents, playing cards or writing letters on their behalf. Some members of the service team drove assisted living residents to restaurants or helped them run errands, but most residents were content with a friendly conversation. The team held a church service on Thursday nights for residents unable or unwilling to leave the home.

Two members of the team had already arrived when Wayne strolled into the event room. The dimly lit facility smelled of urine and filthy mop water, and the faded green walls descended into a broken tile floor. The rest of the group trickled in, buzzing with summer stories. After a brief meeting about the evening service, Wayne stood. "Let's pray and get started," he said.

"I'll do it," said Lewis.

The group of five bowed their heads, and Lewis said a short prayer.

Wayne gave a nod to the events coordinator, and she opened the doors. A dozen residents shuffled into the room. Nurse's aides pushed in a couple more elderly woman in wheelchairs. Within five minutes, over twenty seniors impatiently or indifferently waited for the service to start. A black woman sat front and center wearing a wrinkled red dress with a matching purse. She wore a black hat with a blue flower pattern. A latecomer found a spot in the back and immediately fell asleep.

The events coordinator walked back into the room and nodded at Wayne. He made eye contact with Lewis and nodded. Lewis rose, and the other students followed his lead. Gina stood next to Will in front of the assembly, and Kristen sat at the piano.

"Welcome," said Lewis. "And thank you for coming to this week's service."

After praying, Lewis led the inattentive assembly in a hymn. Gina and Will sang as Will played the guitar. Kristen accompanied on piano. The woman in the red dress stood up from her folding chair to belt out the hymn. Only four other residents sang at all. One of the patients in a wheelchair responded to the music by raising his hands. After three more hymns, Lewis shuffled through his notes. "And now," he said, "it's time for this week's special music."

Will played the guitar while Gina and Kristen sang an upbeat praise song. The woman in the red dress didn't differentiate the duet from the congregational singing. She remained standing and sang louder than Gina or Kristen. The song ended and Gina sat next to Kristen in the front row.

"Thank you, Will and Gina, for our special music," said Lewis. "And now it's time for a sermon from the Word of God."

Wayne grabbed his Bible and stood in front of the distracted room with a friendly smile. "In tonight's sermon I'm going to talk to you about salvation. I'm going to explain what the Bible says about salvation. When we're done you can know for sure that you have eternal life."

Chapter 9

"Okay, boys," said the waitress. "I got one large stack of chocolate chip pancakes."

"That's mine," said Kurt.

"A double cheeseburger with fries?" asked the waitress.

John Paul raised his hand.

"And you must be having the Denver omelet with a small stack of buttermilk pancakes?" The waitress smiled brightly at Elio as she put the last of the entrees in front of him.

Life seemed to come easy for Elio Khoury. His baby face and wide shoulders made him a favorite with the girls, and his six foot three wiry frame made him a natural athlete. Kurt stood just an inch shorter, but he seemed to fall short in every comparison. Elio's future was bright. His Lebanese Father owned eight Jewelry stores in the Dallas area. By the time Elio was a sophomore he had entered a mentor-apprentice relationship with his father to become a master jeweler.

"Does everything look okay, boys?" asked the waitress. She looked to Elio for an answer.

"Can I get some ranch?" asked John Paul.

"Yes, sir, I'll be right back with it." The waitress disappeared into the kitchen.

"So Julie's gone to Florida?" asked Elio.

"Yeah," said Kurt, "she left this morning. I went over to her house last night."

"Did you tell her?" asked Elio. "Did you say anything to her?"

"Nah. What's the point? She's gone. I'll probably never see her again. We're just friends anyway. That's all we'll ever be."

"She'll be back at Christmas or spring break," said John Paul. He plucked a piece of stray bacon off the table and shoved it into his cheeseburger.

"Maybe," said Kurt, "but she'll have a new life by then, new college friends. She won't care about me anymore. Things will never be the same."

Elio finished cutting his omelet into a dozen equal parts and looked up at Kurt. "You've chased Julie since the eighth grade," he said. "You can't just let her go without trying."

"It's not that simple. I've gone down that road a thousand times. We get real close. We're best friends. She can't stay away from me. Everything I say makes her laugh. She looks at me like I'm brilliant. Then I make a move and she says, 'Whoa, hold on. We're just friends.' Or she'll say 'I could never look at you like that. It would destroy our friendship.' Then it's awkward for a few months. Then we start the cycle all over again. At least this way it's over, she's gone, and I don't need to think about it anymore, a burden lifted."

"Good riddance," said John Paul.

"You don't believe that," said Elio, looking at Kurt. "You'll never be over her."

"Like you said, I've chased her since the eighth grade. I had a bunch of chances at girls, but always held out for Julie. What do I have to show for it? One time, our sophomore year, I texted her exactly what I thought of her, everything. She didn't text back or talk to me for two days. Finally, she texted me back and said she was sorry that I had the wrong idea. She said as soon as she read my text she got sick. She literally puked."

"No she didn't," said Elio. "You would have told me that."

"I *did*, three years ago. You just don't remember. It was a bit more memorable to me."

John Paul appeared to be lost in his cheeseburger, oblivious to Kurt's dismay. He finished his burger in less than eight bites, then licked the grease running down the back of his hand. "No one *dates* anymore," he said. "There's no more *girlfriends*. You get some pot and invite her to smoke out and that's it. You're in."

"*I* have a girlfriend," Elio protested.

"Yeah, and next month you'll have another."

While Elio and John Paul conversed, Kurt spread butter over each of his pancakes liberally, covered them in maple syrup, and restacked them.

"I've been dating Marcy for two and a half months," said Elio.

"There's too many girls out there to waste time on any one of them. Hit it and move on." John Paul turned from Elio to Kurt. "You didn't hit it. So what? Move on. It's not just guys. Girls don't even want a relationship anymore."

Kurt and Elio's mouths were too full to contest.

"In Sweden nobody marries anymore," John Paul continued. "Their population is going down because no one wants to have babies."

"I don't live in Sweden," said Kurt

"Maybe it was Switzerland?"

"And I don't care what you or Elio or anyone else does. I'm stuck on Julie and I can't help it. What can I do? The heart wants what it wants."

"Okay, but you're going about it all the wrong way. You know who knows you're hooked on Julie? Julie does. And there's nothing more pitiful to a girl than a guy who worships her. To them it's not romantic or loyal or anything else. It's desperate. She walks all over you and lets you flatter her. But she looks somewhere else for a guy."

"So what do you want me to do, kick her in the shin?"

"Three words; you're the prize."

"Not this again," said Elio.

"Look," continued John Paul. "You think of Julie as the greatest thing you can imagine, but you can't put all your cards on the table. If you let her know she's the prize, she'll act like the prize. Then she'll start thinking she *is* the prize and that she can do way better than you. Even if she keeps you around she'll always have you by the balls."

"But she is the prize," said Kurt.

"Yeah, but you can't let her know that. That's why you've been friend zoned."

"I don't care about prizes, or playing games like that. I just want her."

"There's always games. If you ignore them it just means you're losing."

"Don't listen to him," said Elio with an irritated smile. "He's full of shit."

John Paul Khaled was a phenomenal varsity point guard, but at five foot six his playing days were limited to high school. He drew comparisons to a tiny lumberjack due to his stocky frame and thick beard. His parents moved to Texas from Gaza City, Palestine and opened a gas station months before John Paul was born, and like Elio, John Paul worked for His father. But he refused to work more than thirty hours a week, taking no interest in learning the family business.

"No," said John Paul. "These are facts. I'm not making this shit up. It's science. I'll tell you something else. The next time you talk to Julie, look at her mouth while she talks, just real subtle like. Occasionally look at her mouth. If you look at a chic's mouth when she's talking she pictures herself having sex with you. It's a mental thing. It's science."

"You're so full of it," said Elio. "Where do you get this stuff?"

"I didn't make it up. Google it. It's just the way it is."

"I'm not trying to sleep with her. I mean, yeah of course, I want that, too, but that's hardly top of mind. I just click with her better than anyone I've ever known. I think I love her, and I missed my last chance to tell her."

"Don't talk about love," said John Paul. "Especially when you're talking to Julie. Girls don't want to hear you talk about love. You have this Hollywood idea of love, like in a chic flick. Girls don't want love. They don't want you to tell them you love them. They just want to be desired, a lot. They want you to make them laugh and entertain them. I'm telling you, they don't want love. It's too complicating, too much of a hassle. They don't want to be loved; they want to be liked. All girls are the same. They can't help it. It's biology."

"Whatever," said Kurt. "I don't think you and I are looking for the same thing."

The waitress placed two packets of ranch dressing on the table. "Here ya go, hon," she said and continued on to another table.

John Paul opened a ranch packet and dunked two crinkle cut fries. "Don't you get it?" he said, looking at Kurt. "What turns girls on more than anything else is a guy who's wanted by other hot girls."

"But I'm not wanted by other hot girls."

"It doesn't matter. Look, here's what ya do. The next time you're with Julie—"

"I don't even know if I'll see her again."

"It doesn't matter, Hitz, you'll get over her. The next time you see some girl you want, here's what you do. When you see her coming toward you, turn away from her and snub her as though you don't care and start talking to another girl. And be sure she sees it. This shows that *you* are the prize. You're sending her a message, 'fine, if she's not interested, I've got many other options.' This makes her super jealous, and now she's into you, like she's missing something. And if she texts you, don't go firing off a dramatic response two seconds later. Wait a few hours. Maybe the next day. Then text back a cold but positive response. Now you're in. And don't ever apologize. For anything. It makes her feel too much like the queen."

"Bullshit," said Elio.

"Yeah?" said John Paul. "Then why do I always have girls? I'm juggling three right now."

"Are you counting Helen Bartosiewicz?" asked Elio.

Elio and Kurt both laughed.

"That shit doesn't work," said Elio. "They see right through it. Girls don't like to be played, and they're smarter than he thinks. You might get a date that way, but not with anyone worthwhile. And it won't fool any girl for long. Just relax, Kurt. Just keep it real. That's all girls want."

Kurt looked down at his plate. Keep it real? he thought. I've been keeping it real my whole life. That's gotten me nowhere.

Chapter 10

Ranae continued working the early shift and clocked out each day at noon. She jogged when she got home then studied her thick paperback book until Wayne's return in the early evenings. By the end of September she was poised to attempt the Texas State Nursing Board exam.

Wayne drove her to the test site because she was too nervous to drive. When they pulled into the parking lot her heart lurched.

"This is insane," said Ranae. "I'm a wreck. Why am I so nervous? I'm ready for this."

"Just relax," said Wayne. "In forty-five minutes you'll be done forever."

"Forty-five? It'll probably take me three hours."

"Three hours? You said it took less than an hour."

"Well, it could. There's two hundred questions, but I might not have to answer them all. The computer calculates your score as you go. As soon as you demonstrate a passing or failing grade the computer shuts down and you're done. The minimum number of questions is fifty. The maximum is two hundred. So it could take up to three hours, but I won't know the results for a few weeks."

Ranae returned to the car fifty-eight minutes later. She sat in the passenger seat with a blank face.

"So, how did it go?" asked Wayne as they exited the parking lot.

"I don't know," said Ranae. "It shut off at fifty questions. Exactly at fifty questions."

Wayne drove in silence.

"Is that good or bad?" Ranae asked, looking at Wayne.

Wayne kept his eyes on the road. "Well, how do you think you did?" he asked.

"I either aced it or bombed it big time. At first I thought I was doing well. But then I kept second guessing everything. I don't feel like I did well enough to be done at fifty. But I don't feel like I bombed it either."

The next morning Ranae arrived at the bakery, reviewing the exam in her mind. She looked around Samson's and counted her blessings. The humble bakery had no fussy patients or charting or government red tape. The work was easy because everything came to the store frozen or pre-made, and when frozen bread was baked it smelled just as wonderful as homemade. But she began to wonder if she would be at Samson's much longer than she had planned.

"How is Phoebe doing?" Ranae asked Leslie, as the two stood across a prep table from one another, unboxing yeast rolls.

"Not good," said Leslie. "Not good at all. I doubt if she makes it to the weekend."

"That's awful. I'm so sorry."

"When I left home she was lying on the floor. She couldn't even get out of bed, and she shakes all the time. Mindy put a sausage treat right in front of her nose and she didn't even move."

"What are you going to do?"

"Well, I guess I'll have to put her down. But I really wanted her to make it to the weekend. Bethany's coming home from Knox City. Phoebe's her dog, ya know. She got her for Christmas when she was eight. If she's not here when Phoebe dies she'll be devastated."

"Oh no."

"I've been telling her for weeks to come home."

"Bethany is the middle one, right?"

"Yeah, she lives in Knox City. It's like three and a half hours west. Her boyfriend, Danny, was in a band, but when it broke up they both moved out there. I think he delivers pizzas now. I haven't seen her since Christmas. I hate to say it, but maybe it's a good thing Phoebe's sick. At least it gets Bethany home for the weekend."

"My daddy's from there," said Rodney, pushing a rolling metal cabinet from the front counter. "Well, actually he's from Stamford. It's right next to Knox City."

"You've been to Knox City?" asked Leslie.

"Oh, yeah," said Rodney, pushing the cabinet into a corner. "Lots of times. My granddaddy owns a radio station out there." He walked toward another cabinet full of angel food cakes and pushed it toward the counter.

"A radio station," said Ranae. "He owns his own radio station?"

"Yeah," said Rodney.

Leslie made eye contact with Ranae and shook her head with a sarcastic smile. "What's the name of the radio station?" Leslie asked.

Rodney looked at the ceiling in contemplation. "I don't remember," he said. "It's an AM station. They mostly play country music." Rodney disappeared into the front to put out the cakes.

"He's a lying sack of crap," said Leslie.

"He *might* own a radio station," said Ranae.

"Shoot. Rodney lies about everything, honey," said Leslie. "You think he's telling the truth about a radio station?"

Ranae laughed. "It's possible. He has a nice truck. He must get his money somewhere."

"Yeah," Leslie said, putting her thumb and index finger to her mouth, mimicking the act of smoking. "He must get his money somewhere."

"I took my state boards test yesterday."

"How'd you do? Did ya pass?"

"I won't know for a couple of weeks. I have no idea how I did."

"Oh, I'm sure you passed. But I'm praying you didn't."

"Leslie!"

"No, I don't mean it, honey. I knew the day I interviewed you, we wouldn't have you long. Actually, I shouldn't have hired you, but I couldn't help it."

"I'm not sure how soon I'll be leaving." Exactly fifty questions, she thought.

When Ranae entered the apartment, the light was on in Wayne's office.

"What are you doing home?" Ranae asked. "It's 12:30 in the afternoon." She curled up in Wayne's lap and put her head on his shoulder. Wayne wrapped his arms around her and kissed the top of her head.

"My Rabbit's home," said Wayne. "I hoped you'd get home soon. I had to take off early. I've got two papers due this week and I'm running out of time."

"You didn't come home to see me?" she asked, looking up at Wayne with a fake pouty face.

"You're the bonus." Wayne kissed her, moving his hand up her thigh, then pulled back. "But I really have to get this done."

"I'm starving," said Ranae. "Take me to lunch. Please. I'll leave you alone after that."

"Don't do this to me. I can't."

"Have you eaten lunch yet?"

"No," said Wayne. "And I wasn't planning on it. I'll grab a protein bar."

"I'll take you to that awful sandwich place you love, King, uh, King something."

"Pastrami King. No. Ranae, you're killing me. I've got to finish this paper."

"I'll buy you ice cream." Ranae smiled big, stood, and took Wayne's hand. "Come on," she said. "You have to eat sometime."

Wayne kissed Ranae and walked into the kitchen. He came back with a protein bar in his hand. "Don't worry," he said. "We'll go out this weekend. I promise. But I took off work to catch up. Please, just give me a few hours."

"No promises," said Ranae with a guilty smile. She sat on the sofa and curled up with a Danielle Steel novel.

Wayne shut the office door and sat at his desk. The laptop flashed to life, and he flipped through the pages of a heavily worn paperback copy of *Pensées*. He found the page he was looking for and pored over it for several minutes, pausing occasionally to take notes. He was writing an essay on the Christian apologetics of Blaise Pascal.

Wayne chose Pascal's Wager theory as his paper topic because his theory purportedly allowed Christians the liberty of trusting the Christian faith without the burden of reasonably defending the inerrancy of the Bible.

He had been searching for a way to salvage his faith for years. He desperately wanted to reconcile his heart with his faith, but the more he studied the Bible, the more difficult it became. The Bible introduction class Wayne took as a freshman in Bible College was often called the *weed out* class for pastors. In this class, students learned the process of how the Bible came into existence. The authorship, the original languages, textual criticism, redaction criticism, and formation of the New Testament canon were all discussed in detail.

Kevin Cobb

Wayne had entered Vandyke Bible Institute with the firm belief every word of the Bible was inspired by God and that every word of it had endured to the present time without error. He had made a promise to himself; if I ever discover a single mistake in the Bible, I'm out.

On the first day of Bible introduction class, Dr. Balis proclaimed that the Bible didn't contain one error, rather, it contained over a hundred thousand textual errors. In the next breath he reassured the class that the errors weren't present in the copies of the original autograph manuscripts. The originals were perfect, he had said, but the process of copying the texts over and over again, spanned more than two thousand years. Through the centuries, several small discrepancies and inconsistencies had crept into the manuscripts. Unfortunately, the flawless original texts no longer existed. The important thing to understand, said Balis, is that there are no errors in the remaining copies that affect doctrinal issues. Even The fallen nature of humanity couldn't destroy God's Word.

The professor continued speaking, but Wayne had tuned out. His theological frame of reference was shattered.

He'd been misled his entire life. No errors that affect doctrine, he thought. What does that mean?

Wayne held on to the sliver of hope that he had misunderstood the professor, but this wobbly view of biblical inerrancy was subtly or overtly taught and supported in all of his classes. He learned to use buzz words like *paradox* and *antinomy* to resolve apparent discrepancies in scripture instead of ugly words like *contradiction*. To Wayne, the Christian defense consisted of smoke and mirrors, rather than scholarship. He went to VBI to strengthen his faith, not to become an illusionist.

Wayne continued to study theology, apologetics, and Church history, but with a critical eye, praying constantly that God would restore the faith he had involuntarily lost. The more Wayne studied, however, the less he believed. The roughshod process in which the biblical canon had been established sent him looking for alternative solutions. He appreciated the attempts of modern theologians like Schleiermacher and Barth to respond to the higher criticism generated by the enlightenment, but he believed they threw the baby out with the bath water. They solved the inerrancy problem, but at the cost of traditional Christian doctrine.

Graduation day arrived before Wayne was able to find peace. He applied to seminary because he wasn't trained to do anything but preach. When he entered seminary he was determined to be more active in his faith. His faith had become a matter of thinking rather than serving, he thought, and if he acted like a believer, his faith would surely follow. He increased his involvement at church and started the ministry at Walbrook. Plunging himself into ministry, he continued on with the confidence that God would zap him somewhere along the way and transform him into a sincere Christian.

Wayne's final year of seminary resembled his last year of college. Time was running out and he was still waiting for a divine epiphany. He had just finished reading Locke's *Reasonableness of Christianity*. Locke argued that Christianity is valid because it's the most reasonable of all religions for the common man to understand. Wayne found the argument unconvincing.

Wayne's latest hope was Pascal. Maybe a mathematician had the answer. He sat at his desk reading and re-reading excerpts of Pascal, periodically typing notes on his computer. Ranae abruptly opened the office door wearing nothing but Wayne's Dallas Cowboys jersey.

"I'm ready for a nap," Ranae said, looking at Wayne seductively.

Wayne laughed playfully. "You're killing me here," he said.

"We're, newlyweds. That's what we're supposed to do."

"Let me ask you something. Why do you believe the Bible? How do you know it's the Word of God?"

Ranae's playful smile dropped and was replaced by a look of confusion then contemplation. "I don't know," she said. "I just do. I can't imagine anything else, so I just believe what I know is true." After humoring Wayne with a genuine answer, she returned to her playful mood. She smiled and ran her hands through her hair, then raised the bottom of the jersey high enough to catch Wayne's eye.

"Okay," Wayne said with a smirk. "You win. Just give me another hour."

Ranae extended her hands over her shoulders and grabbed the back of the jersey. She slowly raised the jersey over her hips and past her chest. With a guilty smile, she playfully tossed the Jersey onto Wayne's laptop.

Wayne was done studying.

Chapter 11

Knowing his next scheduled cardiology appointment was less than two weeks away, Steve failed to consult Dr. Dekker about the fishing incident. He also knew, however, his heart was declining quicker than he'd anticipated. With the exception of running, he was still capable of most physical activities, but his recovery time following strenuous activity grew longer. He still biked, though he avoided dirt trails, settling for the smooth asphalt of the suburban neighborhood streets. He walked more persistently, but even the small hills seemed like mountains. Although stairs became his nemesis, he was still capable of climbing large inclines with rest breaks.

Basic household activities, such as gathering trash and showering, became major tasks. One day in the laundry room he transferred a wet load of socks and t-shirts from the washer to the dryer, then filled the washer with a load of shorts. The mundane chore robbed his energy and left him panting. He spotted a stray sock on the floor. When he bent to pick it up, his face glowed a shade of crimson. He became dizzy and leaned against the laundry room wall to catch his breath and regain his equilibrium.

After starting the washer he slid onto the Oak laminate floor to gather enough strength to return the hamper to the bedroom. Steve sat on the floor contemplating the year ahead. Where would he find the strength to match teenage defiance for six class periods a day? How would he stand all day long? How would he coach two sports?

For the first time since Steve's sickness, he reflected upon his congenital heart condition. Steve was born with transposition of the great arteries. This meant his pulmonary artery and aorta had developed in reverse position. Blood circulation is poor in transposition patients, causing their skin to appear to have a blue shade, leading to the nickname, *blue babies*. The condition was fatal before the late 1960's, but as the decade came to a close a new procedure, the Mustard Procedure, allowed blue babies born in the Seventies and Eighties to experience relatively normal lives.

The Mustard Procedure altered the anatomy of the heart, rerouting the walls of the heart to save the patient from certain death, but the alteration placed the majority of the work on the right ventricle, which is naturally weaker than the left. Therefore, a transposed heart repaired by the Mustard Procedure wore out much sooner than a normal functioning heart.

Steve's childhood was relatively normal, but he could not run for long without getting winded. He loved cardio sports like football and basketball, but always struggled to compete with his peers. As a result, he gravitated to baseball.

Andy stopped by one evening to find Steve sitting in his recliner.

"Son! How are you?" Steve said with genuine enthusiasm.

"Good, Dad, how are you feeling this week?"

"I can't believe you're finally here," said Steve abruptly. "I'm in shock. I hope you don't send my heart over the edge. Why don't you ever visit?"

"Sorry, Dad, just busy."

"Five years from now you'll wish you'd spent more time with me. It'll be too late then."

"Don't talk like that. You're going to be fine. Transplants happen every day."

"Well, we'll see about that." Steve looked down in dark contemplation, then up into Andy's eyes. "You know I only live five miles away. Why don't we ever watch Rangers games together or football games on the weekends, or go fishing? I can't take the boat out anymore, but you could take your old man out. But, no. I never see you."

"I'm here *now,* Dad. Why do you always have to spend all of our time together telling me that you never see me? I only live five miles away too, ya know. Why don't you ever visit *me*?"

"When are we going to use that gift certificate I gave you for Christmas? I haven't been deep sea fishing in years."

Andy paused and put his hands in his pockets before before answering. "It's already been used. A couple of weekends ago."

"Oh, you went without me?"

"The gift certificate expired next month, and I knew I wouldn't get a chance to get down to the gulf before then."

Steve's face revealed rejection, but suddenly turned into an amused grin. "So how did you do?" asked Steve. "What did you catch?"

"Well, I didn't actually go myself," Andy said hesitantly. "Phil from work was going to Houston for the weekend, and I knew I wouldn't get a chance before next month, so I gave it to him."

Rage flared in Steve's eyes. "What the hell? Do you know how much that cost me? What a spoiled, entitled little shit I've raised."

"I'm sorry, Dad. I—?"

"If you weren't going to use the gift certificates, you could have given them back. Last time I go out of my way to Christmas shop for you."

"Yeah, I'm sorry. I should have. I'll make it up to you."

Steve stood and walked toward the restroom without looking back. "I've got friends coming over in an hour. I've got to get showered and ready." After Andy left, Steve stepped out of the restroom, poured a glass of Cruzan and Coke, and sat on the Lazy Boy, seething.

On the drive home, Andy reflected upon the transformation his father had undergone since his last visit. He was breathing louder, and he moved slow and deliberately. He's dying, Andy thought. And I couldn't even give him a day of fishing. He's a cantankerous son of a bitch, but he's right. Five years from now he could be gone. Maybe sooner. I can't keep wasting opportunities. Andy resolved to visit his father every week.

At Steve's next appointment, Dr. Dekker noted a sharp decline in Steve's condition. "The x-rays and sonograms indicate that your ejection fraction has dropped to eighteen percent." He said. "When an EF falls below twenty percent we need to implant a defibrillator," said Dr. Dekker. "It's called an ICD."

Steve's parents had cautioned him that he may need a pacemaker later in life. "A defibrillator?" he asked. "You mean a pacemaker?"

"Well, yes, it will also pace, but your heart is susceptible to fatal heart rhythms. In case of a sudden lethal heart rhythm, a defibrillator will immediately reset your heart in a healthy rhythm. It could save your life."

"I know I've been drinking too much. I've been hard on my heart the past couple months. I'll back off, I'll quit. Give me another chance. The next time I come in I'll have my ejection fraction up where it belongs."

Dr. Dekker laughed. "If you quit drinking that would be great," he said. "I recommend it. But your drinking isn't responsible for this. You have congenital heart failure. It's a birth defect, not caused by lifestyle. Your heart is winding down. Nothing you can do will heal it. It's dying. But with medication and a defibrillator we can prolong the process."

On the morning of Steve's surgery, Andy drove him to the hospital. Just before a nurse pushed Steve into the operating room, Andy grabbed Steve's hand and gave him a reassuring smile. "See ya real soon, Dad."

Steve regained consciousness three hours later with Andy by his side. Within an hour Dr. Dekker stopped in. "Very good, Mr. Dunham. The surgery went well."

The left side of Steve's chest ached. Any movement of his left arm made him wince with pain, so he lay still.

"The defibrillator works," said Dr. Dekker, "We tried it out while you were sleeping."

"Tried it out?" Steve repeated. "You mean you shocked me?"

"Yes, we have to test it," said Dr. Dekker with a smirk. "Believe me, you don't want us testing it when you're awake. It feels like you've been kicked in the chest by a mule."

"Well, hell."

"If it's triggered, you need to give us a call immediately. If it's triggered more than once in a day, go straight to the E.R. But hopefully you won't have to experience that." The doctor paused, glanced at Andy, then back at Steve. "Now, we were only able to connect one of the leads because of your odd heart anatomy due to your transposition and related surgeries. The other two leads just wouldn't reach. This isn't a problem. Only one is needed to activate the defibrillator. It just won't pace your heart like we were hoping."

Kevin Cobb

"So how does my transposition affect my chances of getting a transplant?" asked Steve. "I mean, does it prevent me from qualifying for a heart?"

"It shouldn't be a problem. We've never done a transplant on a transposed heart at OLA. It may be a little tricky, but it shouldn't be a problem. Our concern will be whether or not the veins and arteries are long enough to connect to a healthy heart. But the surgeons can use a graph if they need to. Dr. Mino leads the team of surgeons. He's been a part of hundreds of transplants surgeries at the Cleveland Clinic. He's one of the very best in the country."

Dr. Dekker's comments were intended to comfort Steve, but he received the counsel as a death sentence. Steve sensed uncertainty in Dr. Dekker's answer, confirming Steve's greatest fear. A successful transplant was uncertain at best, but realistically, it was doubtful.

Steve was released from Our Lady of Angels the following day soon after the bandages were removed and his left arm was mobile again. He stood shirtless in front of his bathroom staring at the fresh diagonal scar below his collar bone. He had anticipated the defibrillator would be noticeable, but had no idea how prominently it would stick out. It protruded distinctly from his chest, like a jewelry box had been embedded just below his skin.

To Steve, the jutting rectangle represented the first domino in a chain of events that he believed would quickly culminate in a transplant. He associated the transplant with death and was convinced the end was near. His thoughts turned to his daughter. He found a yellow legal pad and began to write:

Hi, Becca. How have you been? I haven't heard from you in so long. Every year I send you a Christmas card and I'm still waiting for a response. I have a pacemaker in my chest now, and a heart transplant is right around the corner. If you want to see your dad alive again you need to come see me now. Time is short. I love you very much, and I hope you come back into my life.

Dad

Steve folded the letter, stuffed it into an envelope, and placed it in the mailbox. He returned to the house, hopeful Becca would respond.

Chapter 12

Wayne knew it would be a large service that night. Thursday nights were usually shared with bingo night at Walbrook, but bingo was canceled that week because Glenda Freeman, the bingo commissioner, had the flu. The church service, therefore, would be the sole entertainment of the night. Attendance would double.

The service team arrived an hour before the service to spend time with residents. Unburdened of her study obligations, Ranae joined the team. Wayne reviewed his sermon notes then walked around the cafeteria, mingling with the residents and team members.

"My sister Bernice died in 1974," Marie told Ranae. "She was killed in a boating accident. I've never seen her kids since." Ranae sat across from Marie, painting the octogenarian's nails with brick red polish. "I think her son James is married," Marie continued. "But he couldn't find a job. Maybe he went back to Brindisi. Of course, I lost my Antonio in 2004. He had colon cancer."

"Antonio was your husband?" Ranae interrupted politely.

"Yes, dear," Marie said with a gracious smile. "We were married sixty-one years. When we were first married he took me to the beach at Case Bianchi. It was less than an hour from our home, but we lived right next to the sea, so why go anywhere else? For a whole week and a day we were there. Antonio got sunburnt badly our first day. So we stayed inside during the day and ate *pettole* with our *sangiovese*. When we weren't eating, we'd make love. We made love all day long, and late at night we would go out onto the beach. We were the only ones out there. We caught sand crabs and threw them at each other. We swam in the moonlight and watched the stars beside a small fire. If still no one was there, we would make love on the beach and fall asleep until the sun woke us up in the morning."

Ranae giggled. "That sounds like heaven," she said. "Why did you ever leave that for America?"

Ranae touched up Marie's ring finger as Wayne shifted his attention to Derek's conversation with Walter, an eighty-two-year-old retired Marine. Derek was the only freshman on the team.

"The Bible says you have sinned and I have sinned," said Derek. He had squared his chair directly in front of Walter's wheelchair, forcing Walter to look aside at the ground in annoyance. "We've all sinned," Derek continued. "We deserve to go to hell. You and I deserve to go to hell and suffer for all eternity. But fortunately for us, God made a way for us to be saved. He sent his son to die on the cross. He died and rose again on the third day. If you believe that and ask God to come into your heart and forgive you..."

Walter's face rested on his chest and he snored lightly. Wayne smiled. He knew Walter was pretending to sleep.

Wayne was sure Derek had a good heart, but his ambition overshadowed his compassion. Wayne saw a younger version of himself in Derek. He didn't attend SMU like the rest of the team. Derek attended Vandyke Bible Institute, Wayne's alma mater. Wayne remembered wielding the same misdirected zeal when he was a fresh ministry student. Steve remembered the pride of walking into the dorm lounge and bragging to his aspiring pastor buddies that he had led an old woman to Christ, or boasting of six decisions for Christ while street witnessing. The inside cover of Wayne's black Ryrie Study Bible was covered with the names of all fifty-six converts he had led in the sinners prayer during college. He had written the names inside his Bible to pray for their growth, but in truth, he marked the conversions as a record of his accomplishments, like a divine bank account.

A thin Hispanic man in his early seventies sat beside Wayne. "Pastor Wayne," the man mumbled. "You've got to save me. You've got to get me out of here. She beats me." The man pointed to a lady in a navy blue pants suit behind the administration desk. "Every day she beats me. You've got to get me out of here."

Manuel Perez cornered Wayne every week to claim abuse. Every week, he accused a different staff member.

"Mr. Perez," Wayne said with a friendly grin. "You know that's not true. Sally is the Events Coordinator. She doesn't even treat you."

"But, Pastor Wayne, she beats me every day. My shins are black and blue. She kicks me."

Wayne cringed anytime someone called him pastor. He was far from becoming a pastor, and at this point he wasn't sure if he should be ministering at all.

"Really?" asked Wayne with a smile. "Maybe I can get you some ice. Let me see your shins."

Mr. Perez turned his legs away from Wayne. "She beats me," he said.

Wayne reached into his pocket, pulled out an unopened pack of 1987 Topps baseball cards, handing it to Mr. Perez. "Here you go. This will make your shins feel better."

"Thank you, Pastor Wayne," said Mr. Perez, standing and walking toward his room, opening the pack of cards like a twelve-year-old boy. Mr. Perez claimed to have played minor league baseball until the age of thirty–one and to have made the big leagues in 1986, but he would never name the team he played for. He collected baseball cards in the hope that he would find a baseball card of himself.

Wayne was elated when he had found a box of thirty-six unopened packs of 1987 Topps baseball cards on EBay. The whole box only cost $24.99. Each time Wayne came to Walbrook he brought a pack for Mr. Perez. Wayne wasn't sure if he had actually played in the majors or not, but he sure liked baseball cards.

Derek had moved on to Iris, a former middle school English teacher. "Do you want to pray with me right now to invite Christ into your life as your personal savior?" Derek asked. Iris politely shook her head.

"Are you sure?" Derek asked with a look of confusion. "Because we can pray together right now and you can know that you'll go to heaven when you die."

"No," said Iris.

"I mean, I'm trying to be as clear as I can. If you want eternal security all you have to—"

"Young man, I've been talking to God my whole life. I was going to church fifty years before you were born."

"Going to church doesn't mean you're saved. In the seventh chapter of the Gospel of Matthew, it says that on the Judgment Day many will say 'Lord, Lord haven't I done several great works in your name,' and the Lord will say to him, 'I never knew you.'"

"Derek," Wayne interrupted. "Could you help me get ready for the service?"

Derek excused himself and walked to the front of the room with Wayne. "What can I do for you?" Derek asked.

"You know, maybe it would be best if you developed a relationship with the residents before you bowl them over with an abrasive speech."

"What? You mean I shouldn't share the gospel? Isn't that why we're here?"

"Yes and no. We're here to serve the residents. The gospel is an important part, but no one will listen to you if they're irritated by you."

"Well, I'm not here to be liked. It's on them if they reject the gospel. My job is to present the gospel clearly. Then it's between them and the Holy Spirit."

"Maybe so, but they have to listen before they can hear. An important part of presenting the gospel clearly is gaining people's trust so that they want to listen. If they choose not to listen, they can't hear."

"Yeah, maybe. But what if that lady died tonight and she never heard the gospel?"

"God knows what Iris needs, right? She's been alive for seventy-eight years. When God wants her to understand, He'll give her the information she needs. Not everything happens instantly. And she said she's been going to church a long time. Listen to her experience with church. Maybe it'll open up a dialogue. Maybe you'll learn something."

Sally approached Wayne and interrupted. "Are you about ready to start?" she asked.

Wayne grabbed his Bible. "Yes. We're ready."

Sally opened the door, and the service team took their places at the front as residents trickled in.

Esther, the black woman wearing the same red dress and blue flowered hat, had already found her spot at the front of the room. Wayne looked at her with utter reverence. How does she do it? he thought.

Esther was as confident in her faith as the day she was baptized, over eighty years earlier. She was the widow of a Pentecostal minister and had been involved with ministry her whole life, yet she had no doubts about the Bible nor her faith.

Wayne gathered the team and prayed that God would bless the service and strengthen the faith of everyone in the room.

Kevin Cobb

Chapter 13

The night after Ranae took the state board exam, she kicked her thick study book under the bed. The impatient period of awaiting exam results had begun. She worked as many hours as Leslie would allow and visited Walbrook multiple times a week to pass the time. She ran to the mailbox with optimism each day, but after a couple of weeks without results, the weed of pessimism grew tall. She resumed her daily study routine with the assumption she had failed.

On a Wednesday in mid-September, she clocked out at the bakery and looked at her phone. Her mother had called from Ohio. She climbed into her car to return the call.

"Hi, sweetie," said her mother.

"Hey, Mom, what's up?"

"I have an envelope here from the Texas State Board of Nursing."

"What? How did *you* get it?"

"It looks like it was sent to your dorm on campus, then redirected back here."

"Seriously? I wrote my new address on the exam forms. Why would they send it to campus? Did you open it?"

"No," said her mom. "Not yet. Do you want me to open it or send it on to you?"

Ranae wanted the results now. Good or bad, she needed certainty, but if she failed, she wasn't in the mood to listen to her mom's conciliation speech. "Open it please," she said. She held the phone to her ear with nervous anticipation.

"You passed, sweetie!"

A rush of exhilaration chilled Ranae's heart and shot up her spine. She was flooded with unspeakable relief. When she got off the phone she called Wayne, but he didn't answer. She sent him a text:

I passed!!! It's over. I'm a registered nurse!

Before she reached home, Wayne's reply had already come through:

> *Congratulations! I knew my Rabbit had passed all along. I am so proud of you. I'm taking you out tonight. I bet you can't wait to tell Leslie.*

An unexpected wave of sadness dampened her exuberance. She had become more emotionally involved with the Samson's staff than she had realized. Leslie had become a loyal friend. She would even miss Rodney. He presented an abrasive façade, but he was a good guy who just wanted attention.

Ranae replied:

> *No way. I'm taking YOU out! You've put up with my spastic anxiety for the past month. I've been planning this for a long time. I'm introducing you to my favorite restaurant.*

Later that evening the Davidsons ate at Gershew's in Highland Park, just six blocks from the Southern Methodist University campus. After their meal arrived, Ranae leaned forward to allow the waft of paella to hit her full in the face. Wayne offered a prayer of sincere thanksgiving, and the joyous feast began.

Twenty-five minutes later, Wayne ate the last bite of his Chilean sea bass. He looked across the table at Ranae. "Do you want dessert?" he asked.

"No," said Ranae. "Not another bite. I can't even finish my mussels." She surveyed the table and took notice of the wine cork the waiter had left on the edge of the table. She stuck her hand into her purse, pulled out a pen, and wrote on the cork:

Wayne and Ranae, A Lifetime of Celebrations

"Here," she said, handing the cork to Wayne. "Tag, you're it. I took you out this time. Now you have the cork. You have to keep it until you take me out for our next big dinner. My parents have done this with a cloth napkin for thirty years. My dad took the napkin from a restaurant on their first date. They still do it. It's so cute. It keeps the passion alive."

Wayne turned the cork in his hand, then looked back at her. "What a great idea. Well, it's a fun idea anyway. I don't think we need to manufacture passion. You're all the excitement I can handle."

"Can you imagine what it'll be like thirty years from now?"

"A thirty-year-old cork? I would guess it'll hold up better than a thirty-year-old napkin."

"No. I mean kids, a house. Maybe grandkids. You'll be my grey-haired pastor hubby by then."

"We'll see about that. I haven't even chosen a thesis topic."

"You don't have time for a thesis; you need to plan our next date.

"Don't be surprised if I bring you back here. This might be *my* new favorite restaurant."

"I'm not complaining. I'd come back here every night."

"What do you want to do this weekend?" asked Wayne.

"Anything you like," she said.

"Let's celebrate."

"We are celebrating."

"No, I mean let's get out of town. Let's go somewhere."

"Where can we go? We're still broke. Besides, you're preaching at church Sunday night. We could do something close like Deep Elum? Six Flags?"

"No, not far enough. Let's get out of town. I can get Derek to fill in Sunday. He's always looking for a chance to preach."

The waiter approached the table and laid the check holder on the table.

"Camping," said Wayne. "Let's go camping. We haven't been camping since last spring with your Ohio friends."

Ranae beamed. "Yes!" she said. "Camping."

The Davidsons packed Wayne's Honda on Friday evening and drove two hours to Caddo Lake State Park. They hastily pitched their campsite to get in a quick bike ride before sundown. The winding trail began two miles from their campsite and immediately plunged down a gorge trough a heavily wooded ravine. Navigating the series of speedy switchbacks became a bonsai run evoking laughs and adrenaline. Upon reaching the bottom, however, the trail ascended the rocky chasm with equal severity. The demanding climb was marked by panting and a frantic dash to reach the trailhead in the waning twilight. Using their cell phones as flashlights, the newlyweds escaped the grip of nightfall and found the road leading back to the campsite.

An hour later a campfire crackled and nocturnal forest creatures reverberated on all sides. They sat alongside the fire facing each other in lawn chairs. Ranae looked at Wayne, his solemn eyes staring deeply into the fire.

"Why so serious?" asked Ranae, playfully kicking Wayne's leg. "We're celebrating, remember?"

Wayne broke his gaze and turned to Ranae with a superficial smile. "Sorry, just tired. Just thinking of school, I guess."

Ranae moved to Wayne's chair and curled up in his lap. "Don't think about school. Think about me."

Wayne made a valiant attempt to change his mood. "How could I think of anything but you?"

Ranae looked deeply into his eyes. "Wayne, what's wrong?

"Wrong? Nothing's wrong. It's so peaceful out here. This is great."

"You look like someone's just died. What's wrong?"

"Nothing. You know me. This is as relaxed as I get."

"Babe, you worry too much. Everything we've wanted is happening. I passed my test, and I'll soon be making decent money. We barely put a thousand dollars on the MasterCard, and we'll pay it off real quick."

"I'm not worried about money. I know it will all work out."

"Well, I'm not the only one starting a career. You'll soon be applying to churches. Our life is coming together." Ranae placed a kiss on his forehead and several on his neck. "Besides," she said, "none of that matters anyway. We found each other. We have fifty years of playful romance and mind-blowing sex to look forward to. Just you and me. I'll kiss you when you're bald, and you'll make love to me when I've got long white hairs on my neck. When our kids check us into Walbrook I still won't be able to keep my hands off of you."

"You're right," said Wayne. "Everything is more than great. Perfect even."

Ranae pulled her head back to look at Wayne.

"I guess that's what scares me," he said. "Anytime things are going great in life, I'm always afraid disaster is right around the corner. Many a slip twixt cup and lip."

"What does that mean?"

"It's an old proverb. It kind of means, don't count your chickens before they hatch. In ancient Greece there was this guy named Anacaeus, or so the story goes."

Ranae rested her head on Wayne's shoulder and gently rubbed his chest over his button-down shirt.

Wayne continued, "Anacaeus claimed that he had the best vineyard in Greece. A soothsayer from his village prophesied Anacaeus would die before he tasted the wine of his beloved vineyard. Anacaeus laughed at the soothsayer, but just as he was about to take the first sip of wine from the vineyard, he was called by his servants to hunt a wild hog that was running loose in the vineyard. He set his cup down and ran to defend his winery. He was killed in the chase and never took a sip of the wine. Many a slip twixt cup and lip. It means don't get too confident in your success; the tables may turn when you least expect it. Things are going so well, too well. With you, with us, with me. It's just too perfect."

"Are you kidding? Come on, babe, drop the defeatist attitude. You're freaking yourself out with that kind of thinking. You're freaking me out. Let's just enjoy each other. Life is here now. Relax and enjoy it. God has everything under control. Whatever comes next is fine by me. As long as we're together I can endure anything."

Ranae began unbuttoning Wayne's shirt. "It's getting a bit too cold out here for you to be shirtless," she said. "We better get into the tent." Wayne acquiesced to Ranae's invincible optimism and lost himself in her impeccable charm. He stood to spread the dwindling embers and Ranae sauntered to the tent, removing her own shirt and giggling. "Brrr," she said. "I need your warmth." The coals dimmed and crumbled to ash as the affectionate couple rustled and nestled themselves to sleep.

When Wayne awoke it was still dark. He hoped the sunrise was near because he knew he was awake for the day. His cell phone read 3:49. He stared at a water stain on the blue plastic roof, listening to the dueling hoots of a pair of great horned owls through the ubiquitous clicking of cicadas. Pascal is no better than the rest, Wayne thought. Pascal's Wager is intriguing, but ultimately it does me no good.

Wayne quietly exited the tent and opened the White Yeti cooler they had received as a wedding gift. He pulled out an oatmeal pie and closed the lid. The three raccoons to the left of the tent didn't recoil at Wayne's sudden appearance, but remained frozen where they stood. Even when he pointed the flashlight at them they didn't flinch, but crept slowly backwards in unison. He walked to the bayou where it formed a pond and continued to the end of a long pier and sat, his feet dangling toward the dark water. A lone spotlight at the end of the pier highlighted a twenty foot diameter section of the bayou.

Caddo Lake is the only natural freshwater lake in Texas. All other Texas lakes are man-made reservoirs. It's believed that an earthquake in the early 1800's formed the twenty-six thousand acre lake straddling the Texas-Louisiana border. Two hundred years later the lake is overgrown with lively mature cypress trees rising right out of the water.

The spotlight was powerful, yet too small to illuminate the vast body of water beyond a few hundred feet. Everywhere Wayne looked, large cypress trees emerged from the lake, their leaves dancing to a gentle breeze against a brilliant, star-filled sky. He removed the oatmeal pie from the wrapper and shoved it into his shorts pocket.

He had spent the past week studying Pascal's theory, *The Great Wager*, both analyzing and evaluating it. He personalized the theory to see if Pascal offered him any relief.

I can't prove Christianity with reason and logic, Wayne thought, summarizing the theory, and God can't be discounted by reason. So, every human is obligated to make a wager. I must choose, either God *is* or He *is not*; everyone consciously makes one choice or the other. The rewards of this life are finite while the rewards of an afterlife are infinite. If I believe in God I'll wager with a life of faith. If God exists, I'll receive the infinite reward of eternal life. If God doesn't exist, I've lost nothing. Christianity isn't physically harmful; therefore, even if God doesn't exist, I'm no worse off for living a Christian life. So, according to Pascal, choosing Christianity is the safest bet.

Kevin Cobb

Wayne noticed a dozen or so brim searching for bugs in the beam of the spotlight. Between bites, he pulled off a few oatmeal crumbs and flung them into the water. The tiny fish were too timid to eat from the surface. As each crumb became waterlogged and sank, however, the brim snatched the crumbs before they fell six inches below the surface.

If I choose not to believe in God, Wayne thought, I have the freedom of living my own life free of guilt or religious obligation, but if I'm wrong, I will receive an infinite punishment.

Wayne pulled off another piece of oatmeal, laid it on the dock, and ate the last bite. He flicked his fingers and mini crumbs showered the water. The emboldened brim ate the crumbs upon contact with the surface.

Therefore, Wayne thought, living for an infinite reward, Heaven, is more reasonable than living for a finite reward, Earth. Wayne watched the fish racing to and fro as he critiqued Pascal's theory. Pascal starts with the assumption that God's existence is proof of Christianity, thought Wayne. He assumes that God's existence is synonymous with proof of Christianity, the Christianity derived from the Bible. His theory doesn't *transcend* the reliability of the Bible; it *assumes* it. This may have come as some comfort in seventeenth century Europe, but it does nothing for me. His theory avoids my problems with biblical reliability, the one thing I'm struggling with. Everything we claim to believe about God comes from the Bible. Why can't we defend it without circular reasoning?

Wayne grabbed the remaining oatmeal and broke off smaller crumbs, dropping them into the water. He longed for his high school days when his faith was pure and simple. He knew God was in control, he knew the Bible was pristine. Heaven and hell was as real as the ice cream truck. All was right with the world.

Pascal's theory fell flat, but Wayne remembered a portion of the wager that resonated with his quandary. Pascal gave advice to Christians who *wanted* to believe, but couldn't. Pascal claimed it was of the utmost importance that a doubter be aware of his or her own disbelief so that he or she could relentlessly convince oneself to believe and pray before it was too late. Wayne laughed. Fake it till you make it, he thought. Blaise recommended Wayne's torturous lifestyle over three hundred years ago. Although peace continued to escape Wayne, still he prayed.

"Lord," Wayne said aloud, breaking the peaceful summer night, "heal my lack of faith. I'm exhausted by this journey. I'm disgusted with being a hypocrite. I want to believe. With all my heart I want to believe. I just can't make it all make sense. Please, Lord, I beg you. I'm so uncertain who you are. Make it clear."

Wayne stood and walked back to the tent. He snuggled up to Ranae and found himself staring at the water stain on the blue plastic roof once again. One more quote from Pascal came to mind; "They profess a religion for which they cannot give a reason."

Chapter 14

Steve had dreaded the defibrillator because he feared it would restrict his motion and prevent him from staying active. After the pain associated with the surgery dissipated, however, he generally forgot about the defibrillator's existence.

He rode his bike every morning and took a short walk before bed. The time immediately following exercise was his favorite when his lungs opened and allowed him to fully breathe. The strong palpitations in his chest brought Steve great satisfaction. This false sense of vitality deceived him into believing he was healthy and allowed him to temporary escape his declining health.

True to the promise he had made to himself, Andy visited Steve each of the first three Wednesdays following Steve's surgery. Andy waited tables at Red Lobster and usually had Wednesdays off. On the fourth Wednesday, however, he covered a shift for a co-worker and didn't visit Steve until Saturday morning. When he entered Steve's living room, his father sat cross-armed in his Lazy Boy staring fixedly at the television.

"Well, if it isn't the prodigal son," said Steve.

"Hey, Dad," said Andy. "Sorry about Wednesday. A busy week at work. How was your week?"

"Nobody visited me; pretty boring. It was just me, working, sitting here, watching TV."

"Well, I'm here *now*, Dad. Cheer up."

"What's it been? Like a month?"

"Again? We're going to do this again? I see you as often as I can, way more often than I used to. Sometimes I just can't get away. You could always stop by my place, you know."

"Hm."

"Since I'm the only one who visits, you should be a little more appreciative."

"I wish your sister would stop by. She only lives in Dallas. She never calls, she never texts. Hell, I send her a Christmas card every year. She never sends me anything."

"Becca's busy. Her job's very demanding. Besides, if she called, you'd just criticize her for not calling more often."

"I just don't know what I've done to deserve being ignored by her."

Kevin Cobb

Chapter 15

When Becca was born, Steve beamed with pride. She was his princess, and he spent more time with the baby than he did with Veronica. He vowed to never allow a boy within two miles of her and spoiled her at every opportunity. Veronica was jealous of the bond he and Becca had formed, which rivaled a mother daughter connection. But Steve's infatuation with his baby girl was short-lived. As Veronica recovered from Andy's delivery, her husband's affections turned from her and Becca toward a redheaded study partner he met in college. She and Steve began studying together whenever Steve was on campus. One day she invited Steve off campus for lunch. The next week she invited him to her apartment for lunch. The next week he moved into her apartment.

Steve left the redhead within a year but made no attempt to visit Becca or Andy. He was certain Veronica would prevent him from seeing the children, and he assumed they were too young to remember him anyway.

Kevin Cobb

Each Christmas eve, he stopped by Veronica's to sit with the kids for an hour. This was the extent of his visitation.

The autumn following Steve's college graduation, he began teaching high school American History in the Irving school district to support himself through graduate school, but the forty-five minute commute from Irving to Denton took its toll on his motivation. He took two classes the first semester and just one the second. When the school year ended, he dropped out of grad school and embraced the life of a high school teacher.

Meanwhile, Veronica had met someone new. Jake was four years younger than Steve. He owned a successful landscaping business and drove a red Corvette, but what Steve hated most was the fact that Jake was a great guy.

Steve's kids loved Jake. He was patient and gentle and often took Andy and Becca out for ice cream. He took them on weekend ATV camping trips and played X-box with them for hours on end. Andy constantly asked to see the giant tattoo on Jake's back of a naked Princess Leia climbing out of R2D2. Steve hoped Jake was a passing phase, a Christmas toy that quickly loses its luster, but

Veronica knew she had found a keeper. Eight months after they met they were married.

Steve began the legal process of acquiring visitation rights for Becca and Andy the week after Veronica's Cabo San Lucas wedding. He was granted one weekend a month. Although Andy accepted Jake, he recognized an unbreakable bond between himself and his biological father. The more indifference Steve showed Andy, the more he sought Steve's attention and approval. This paternal bond, so dear to Andy, was foreign to Becca. She regarded Jake as her only father and dreaded Steve's visitation, counting the minutes till she could go home. Andy relished the visits.

The affection Steve received from Andy was overshadowed by Becca's repugnance of him. Steve made numerous attempts to win her over, letting her select restaurants and buying her favorite music CD every time he saw her. The more he pushed, however, the deeper into her shell she crawled. Steve interpreted Becca's disdain as a personal affront, prompting him to design a more extreme scheme to win her over.

147

Kevin Cobb

Steve called Mallory Staley and asked her out on a date. Mallory Staley was the most coveted elementary teacher in the school district. Becca was currently in Ms. Staley's fifth grade class at John Neely Elementary School. Her name was synonymous with teaching excellence throughout the community. Parents competed aggressively to get their children into her class. When Becca had learned Ms. Staley would be her teacher, she eagerly awaited the end of summer, counting the days till the beginning of the school year.

Mallory was thirty-one years old with straight tawny hair and a perpetual smile. She was unassumingly attractive and socially adept, but she rarely dated. She was a natural teacher, but her tremendous success came as a result of her diligent work ethic. Each night she tirelessly prepared for the following school day and the upcoming week. Whatever spare time remained was absorbed by Stella, her ailing mother. Mallory had moved into her mother's house the previous summer when Stella's fight with breast cancer took a severe downturn. On the rare occasion Mallory had an evening of leisure, she curled up with her Kindle and a British classic.

Steve met Mallory the year he started teaching in the district. The superintendent created an initiative to bridge an acrimonious divide in the district by pairing up different grade levels at different schools within the district in a joint project. The superintendent assigned each high school teacher to a middle or elementary school teacher to collaborate in a community project.

Mallory and Steve met multiple times to develop a plan, creating a community clean-up day. They researched the safest, yet dirtiest areas of town to retrieve trash in parks and along roads. Two weeks into the planning the superintendent's initiative was cancelled after several elementary teachers refused to expose their students to the behavior of high school students. The two soon lost contact, but when Steve called Mallory out of the blue for coffee, his invitation was happily received.

On a hot Saturday afternoon in September, the two met at Starbucks. Steve listened thoughtfully as Mallory explained the seriousness of her mother's illness and cheerfully detailed the new math curriculum she had recently implemented. She tried to laud Becca's performance in class, but he redirected the subject back to Mallory. They stood to leave, and he apologized for taking her away from her mother, assuring her that if they decided to see each other again he would come to Mallory's house so that Stella wouldn't be left alone.

The couple spent most of their subsequent dates watching Netflix with Stella. Steve befriended Mallory's fragile mother and even volunteered to take her to doctor appointments. Mallory was smitten by Steve's gracious spirit and caring disposition. She made a spot in her busy life for Steve.

The novice couple kept their relationship a secret until their unlikely engagement in November. When Becca heard the news, her delicate world was flipped upside-down and crashed in front of her. The best part of her life was destroyed by the worst.

Veronica showed up at Steve's front door in a fury. "No!" pleaded Veronica. "You can't marry her goddamn teacher! Absolutely not! This is between you and me. Go find the youngest, sluttiestest girl that will tolerate you and marry her, not Becca's teacher! I know you can't be mature about this, but leave Becca out of it. I didn't marry Jake to one-up you. We just fell in love. You should try it."

"What are you talking about?" retorted Steve calmly. "I've known Mallory for years. Long before Becca was in her class. This has nothing to do with Becca, or you. And it has nothing to do with Jake. It's no one's business but ours."

"You can't put Becca in the middle of this. Becca will be in Ms. Staley's class for the rest of the school year. You can't do this. It'll kill her."

"I have no idea what you're talking about. Look, you don't have to worry. I'm not going to contest the kids' custody. But if Becca wants to start coming over more often, I'd sure appreciate if you'd encourage her."

"No! You son of a bitch! You can't do this! You can't charm Becca's teacher to impress her. You know as well as I do, you'll lose interest in Becca, you'll lose interest in Ms. Staley. You always do, you know this. She'll be humiliated at school. Just let me talk to Becca for

you. I'll put my feelings aside and help her open up to you.
I'll help her to appreciate you. Just don't do it like this."

"Veronica," Steve said calmly, "I understand your
suspicions, but years have passed, I've matured. Finding
the right one was painful for you, and I'm sorry, but now
I've found the right one. Because of my past, I won't try to
convince you differently, but in time you'll come to see
I've changed. Becca is about to have two loving families."

Veronica looked askance at Steve. "I wish I could
believe you, but you've never given me one reason to trust
you. Ever."

"You'll see."

Becca spiraled into a cavernous depression. The
most anticipated school year ever had been invaded by her
deadbeat dad. It didn't take long, however, before she
experienced the fringe benefits of being the teacher's step-
daughter.

The Monday after the wedding, Ms. Staley
announced cheerfully to the class she had married Becca

Dunham's father and from now on she would no longer be called Ms. Staley. From that day forward she wanted to be called Mrs. Dunham. Becca already thought of Ms. Staley as a second mother, but now it was true.

Becca relished her new role as the object of envy by her classmates. Just a few weeks prior, she had been competing with the rest of her class for the right to clean Miss Staley's whiteboard. Suddenly, Miss Staley was driving her home. This new status catapulted Becca to the top of the fifth grade social ladder, and the faculty treated her with unprecedented respect.

Becca cautiously admired the way her father treated Miss Staley and Stella with compassion. She had never seen this side of her father and she saw what her mother had once seen in him. Still, she longed for him to take a similar interest in her, to actually get to know her. Steve never talked to Becca about any subject deeper than school or television.

In time, Becca came to believe he didn't want a relationship with her at all; he only wanted a cheerful daughter to tell him that he was a great father. He wanted a picture of himself with his smiling son and daughter to display on his desk, not a complex relationship requiring daily maintenance.

Despite these reservations, Becca accepted the good with the bad. Steve made Andy happy and brought her closer to Ms. Staley. That was worth something.

By the fifth month of the marriage, however, Steve was hedging his bet. He came to view Mallory as dull and predictable. He was tired of her in the kitchen, the living room, and the bedroom. Stella's health had waned further, and she needed constant care. Mallory hired a home health nurse to visit Stella twice a week, and she took turns with Steve taking off work to take her to appointments. Steve started coaching baseball that spring just to get out of the house and away from the family.

Steve's aspirations of teaching in a university were slipping away; instead, he found himself playing house. He applied to Duke Graduate School in Renaissance history with the hope of taking online classes toward a PhD. He was denied admittance, but was invited to take a single summer class on the Duke campus. On the last day of the Alexandria school year, Steve packed a single suitcase and left Mallory for Durham, North Carolina.

Mallory was blindsided and totally confounded by Steve's clandestine departure. She couldn't bring herself to return to school with Becca in the same building, and her anxiety was compounded by Stella's declining condition. She resigned her teaching position to teach online classes through an agency. Word spread quickly through John Neely Elementary that Becca's father had deserted Ms. Staley, who ignominiously bore the name Mrs. Dunham.

The beloved Ms. Staley was gone, and Becca Dunham was the only one left in the school to shoulder the blame. Becca's trust had been betrayed, and the price was costly. The summer was a nightmare of isolation, and the beginning of the following school year was unbearable. Her sixth grade teacher, Ms. Johnson, was Mallory's best friend. She did little to protect Becca from the cruelty of

155

her fellow students who relentlessly reminded her of her father's scandalous disappearance. Becca sank into a yawning hole of depression beyond the reach of Veronica and Jake. Mercifully, they removed Becca from John Neely and sent her to a private school.

Steve's escape to North Carolina didn't go as planned. He earned a B- in the summer English Reformation class and was denied acceptance into the doctoral program once again. Delays and complications prevented his Texas teaching certificate from transferring to North Carolina. Alternatively, he coached a select baseball team during the summer and substitute taught in the fall. He was allowed to take a second class at Duke, but before Christmas arrived he received a third rejection letter for the fall semester. With his certification issues still unresolved, he packed and headed back to Dallas, taking a job at the Alexandria School with the plan of returning to a public school the following year.

Upon returning to Dallas, Steve insisted Veronica allow him to resume visitation weekends. Andy agreed begrudgingly, but Becca refused to go. Steve forced the issue in court and retained the right to resume monthly visitation. Veronica pleaded with him to spare Becca further scarring by forcing visits, but Steve would not be persuaded.

The first weekend with the kids, Andy was quiet, but cordial. Becca refused to talk. Several visits later she had still not spoken a word. During an April visit, however, Steve recognized a ray of optimism when Becca willingly jumped into his truck without her usual delay tactics. Andy confided in Steve that Becca was mad at her mother for taking her phone away for the rest of the grading period. She had brought a C- home in Science class on a progress report.

Steve recognized an opportunity to gain an advantage. He drove the children to a wireless phone store and asked Becca to pick any phone she liked. Becca silently searched the inventory laden walls of the store and pointed to a phone she wanted. The sales rep removed the phone from the display and began to explain the features and monthly packages.

"I'll gladly buy it," said Steve to Becca. "I'll take care of the monthly charges and everything, but first I want to hear your beautiful voice. Can you tell me thank you?"

Becca said nothing, but stared blankly at Steve.

"Come on, honey, I'm putting out a lot of cash for this phone. I deserve one little sentence. How about one word?"

Becca said nothing. The sales rep handed the phone to Steve and directed them to find him when they decided on a phone.

"Now, Becca," said Steve in frustration. "If you want this phone, you're going to give me one word. Just one word."

Becca said nothing, but continued staring probingly, into Steve's eyes. Eleven-year-old Andy passively observed the standoff.

"Becca!" Steve said firmly, "I'm your father; you have to talk to me. Knock this crap off and start talking. Now!"

Becca sat down cross-legged on the carpet in the middle of the store. She closed her eyes and put her hands over her ears.

Steve looked around the room in embarrassment. His verbal outburst had already seized the attention of the shoppers in the small wireless showroom. They had stopped talking and raptly anticipated a resolution. Steve leaned close to Becca's left ear and said in a fake whisper, "Get up now. Everyone is staring at you." Becca didn't move. "Get up!" Steve screamed. He lightly took hold of her shoulders in an attempt to lift her to her feet.

Becca took her hands off her ears, opened her eyes, and scanned the showroom. Steve released her shoulder, presuming she had come to her senses. Employees and customers alike watched in uncomfortable silence. Her gaze returned to Steve, and she let out a loud protracted scream. The effusive shriek filled the room with amplified uneasiness. Becca went totally limp and assumed a look of tranquility. She lay face-up on the beige carpet with her eyes half open. The thirteen-year-old girl looked outrageously long spread out on the small showroom floor.

Steve was paralyzed by her audacity. He took a deep breath and let it out with a sigh. "Get up, honey," he said, defeated. "We're going home."

Becca stood immediately and gained eye contact with Steve one last time. She smiled a most angelic smile as she moved past him. She exited the store and sat in the truck. Steve drove straight to Veronica's and dropped off the siblings without saying another word. The next time Steve picked up Andy for a visit, he accepted Becca's absence without protest.

Chapter 16

Although Steve noticed a marked change in his condition, he still preferred activity to idleness. Cycling was his preferred exercise. The speed, the wind, and the freedom brought him to life and provided a temporary escape.

Steve's neighborhood sat atop a half mile long hill. At the bottom was Chancellor's Green, a beautiful semi-wooded park with a twenty acre lake and miles of concrete trails.

On a cool October morning he approached the bottom of the hill to begin his ascent home. He was determined to reach the top with three stops or less. He negotiated the rise slowly and steadily. With deep concentration on his breathing, he cleared his usual stopping point with ease. A large oak tree stood along the road more than halfway to the top. Fifteen yards before he reached the tree his legs grew sluggish, and he struggled to catch his breath. The bike inched forward with great reluctance, but he was committed to passing the mighty oak before putting a foot on the ground.

He climbed off the bike with great satisfaction at the base of the tree. He sat on the curb and raised his hands above his head to open his burning lungs. The deep breathing brought a sense of health to his lungs, the unmistakable sensation of life. He looked below and saw a man on a touring bike charging up the hill. The lean rider didn't even decelerate as he passed, but smiled and nodded before continuing over the hill and beyond the horizon. The white haired cyclist was no less than sixty years old.

"Son of a bitch," Steve mumbled to himself. After two more bitter stops, Steve topped the crest. Upon arriving home, he stepped off the bike and shoved it against the garage wall. He poured a glass of Cruzan and Coke and crashed in the recliner.

Before summer football camp had concluded, Coach Sturm noticed Steve's deteriorating condition and unsuccessfully petitioned the school to hire an additional coach to lighten Steve's load. When his request was promptly denied, the head coach approached twenty-one-year-old Frank Loxley with the proposition of assisting the team.

Frank had graduated from Alexandria three years earlier and moved back to the Irving area after a year of college. He'd been the starting running back and middle linebacker for Alexandria. His understanding of football far exceeded Steve's, and Frank was thrilled to have a significant role on the football team.

Frank began the season as the assistant offensive coordinator, but by the second week of the season he traded coaching duties with Steve and took the lead in running the offense. Frank thrived in his new role, and Steve was relieved to take a back seat to his former student. This new situation allowed Steve the freedom of leaving practice early. By mid-season he usually attended less than three practices a week.

The Alexandria Panthers played Wheeler Street Christian Academy in the final game of the season. As the players warmed up on the field, Coach Sturm approached

Frank on the sidelines. "Coach Loxley," he said. "Nobody's put the goal post pads on. Can you grab a freshman to help you get those on?"

Before Frank could accept the request, Steve stepped in. "I got it, Coach," said Steve. "Frank's about to walk through the offense. I'll get it."

"Thanks," said Frank, turning to gather the offence.

Steve pulled Mel Blair, the five foot two freshman, out of a warm-up drill. Mel occupied the final spot on the roster. They walked off the field through the west end zone, down a short hill to the small equipment shed.

Steve unlocked the door and turned on the light. After pushing some extra helmets out of the way, he bent over and dragged two large red pads out of the corner. Each pad was longer and bulkier than Mel. Steve stood in a dizzy fog, resting his left hand on the wall for stability. Mel noticed Steve's distressed countenance.

"Coach," said Mel. "Are you okay? Your face is beet red."

Steve breathed deeply for several seconds before answering. "I'm fine, it's just my heart. This is normal." Steve paused for several more breaths before he placed his left foot on one of the pads and slid it to Mel. "You take one, I'll take the other." They ascended the hill in silence. Mel carried a pad on his shoulder, and Steve drug the other behind. When they returned to the west end zone, Mel continued to walk toward the east end zone.

"I'll get the far one," said Mel.

"No," said Steve stubbornly. "I'll get it. You get the close one so you can get back to warm-ups."

"You sure?"

"Yeah, go on." Steve stopped and dropped the bulky pad to catch his breath. Regathering the pad, he lumbered toward the opposite goal post. He stopped to rest three more times before passing the opposite twenty yard line. During the last stop, he took a knee in the midst of the Wheeler Street passing tree. He put his hands behind his neck to open his lungs, fearing his defibrillator would be triggered. A Wheeler Street player noticed Steve's violent breathing.

"Sir, are you okay?" the player asked Steve.

The unwanted attention jarred Steve, impelling him to stand. He still couldn't speak, but nodded to the young man and completed the journey. He laid the pad next to the post and dropped to his knees. He turned around and sat heavily against the field goal post. Whenever he had difficulty breathing he felt like he was inhaling through a coffee straw. The hypothetical straw suddenly seemed kinked.

The Alexandria bench appeared to be miles away. He knew he couldn't make it that far, or even stand. Damn it, he thought. Already? It hasn't even been a year. How can this be happening already?

The Wheeler Street player who spoke to Steve never took his eye off him. When Steve sat in the end zone, the player went to his side-line and pointed out Steve to his coach. The Wheeler Street coach grabbed his trainer and ran out to assist Steve. Alexandria's coaching and training staff soon followed. An ambulance was summoned, and Steve was rushed to OLA.

Kevin Cobb

Chapter 17

As Kurt turned left on Coyote Run Road, he increased his pace. He could see his house through the Pecan trees and the white-fenced cattle field beyond. He was finishing a nine mile run. His feet ached, but his legs remained strong. He read 12:47 a.m. on his watch and calculated his sub-eight minute pace. The Dallas Marathon was less than three weeks away, and he was right where he wanted to be.

Kurt was often jeered by his friends for wearing unorthodox athletic wear when he ran. He was comfortable running in jeans and whatever shirt he happened to be wearing that day. A light jacket or sweater usually sufficed in late November, but a rare northern breeze rolled in earlier that evening. The bitter wind threatened to penetrate even the thickest hoodie. Instead, he wore the closest thing he had to a winter coat, his brown leather jacket and a thick green beanie.

Although the frigid and whistling gale stunned the native Texan, he preferred enduring the cold to running at the community center. He joined the center in September on the premise that the indoor running track would provide the most consistent running environment, but the first time he ventured onto the second-story running surface he was underwhelmed by the width and length of the short oval. At seventeen laps a mile, he needed to run more than eighty tedious laps to complete a productive run.

The short track was two-lanes wide, each flowing in opposite directions like a two lane country road. The inside lane was designated for walkers, the outside for runners. More than two dozen runners, joggers, and walkers occupied the track at any given time; most were elderly walkers, just trying to stay active. Every time a walker passed another runner, he or she had to enter the runners' lane to complete the pass, forcing runners to constantly dodge passers-by or abruptly stop to prevent collisions. Two weeks of swimming against the tide convinced Kurt that heat, cold, or rain was a welcome alternative.

Kurt loped down the middle of the deserted country road, a horse ranch to the left, a cattle pasture, previously owned by his family, to the right. He passed an aluminum watering trough along the inside of the horse fence and broke into a mad dash to finish strong. Although the stinging night air chaffed his cheeks, the sprint was his favorite part of the run.

When he passed the end of the cattle fence, he crossed the lawn, curling in toward the ranch house thirty yards off the road. Kurt leapt onto the porch and collapsed on the bench swing to catch his breath. A cat stood and stretched upon his arrival, leisurely moving across the porch to greet Kurt. A car coming from the same direction Kurt had come squealed its brakes in front of the house, loudly skidding to a stop. Kurt squinted as a blinding spotlight found him on the porch.

Kurt knew who it was. The only question was whether John Paul was alone or if Elio was in the car with him. John Paul had recently mounted a police spotlight onto his Toyota.

Kurt stood, placing his right hand above his eyes to shield the glaring light. "John Paul?" he called out.

Kurt abruptly found himself lying face-down on the porch with a large weight on his back. His arms had been pulled behind him, and he heard handcuffs clasping and tethering his hands together. The cat retreated to the safety of the fallow corn field.

"Where are you going?" asked a police officer.

Kurt was speechless. What does he mean? Kurt thought. I was just sitting here on my own porch swing. "I'm not going anywhere," said Kurt, still attempting to catch his breath.

"What are you doing here?" asked a female voice.

"I live here."

"You live here, huh?" asked the female officer. "Where have you been tonight?"

"I, I was jogging."

"In jeans and a leather jacket?" asked the male officer.

"Yeah, it's cold. I live right here." Kurt nodded toward the house.

"I'm sure you do," said the female officer sarcastically.

"I do!" Kurt screamed desperately. "Ask my mom, she's right in there!"

"You *live* here?" asked the male officer, dubiously.

"Yes! Knock on the door! She's right there, she'll tell you."

"I need to see your ID," said the male officer,

"I don't have it, I was just jogging. It's in my room. Knock on the door, she'll get it for you."

The two officers looked at each other with confusion. "Have you been driving a black BMW tonight?" asked the male officer.

Kurt was dumfounded by the question. He didn't have a BMW, and he hadn't left the house all day. "No," Kurt answered cautiously.

"What's your name?" asked the male officer.

"Kurt Hitzges."

The male officer looked pensively at Kurt. "Put him into the car and let's figure this out," he said to the female officer. She led Kurt to the cruiser twenty feet up the gravel driveway.

The officers conferred for a moment, then climbed the porch. Before they knocked on the door, the female officer noticed something on the bottom porch step. They both crouched to investigate.

Kurt sat in the back of the cruiser, his head spinning, trying to piece together what had happened.

Rather than knock on the door, the female officer returned to the police cruiser and opened Kurt's door. "Sir, are you bleeding anywhere?" she asked.

"Well," said Kurt, as he patted a spot on his forehead. "I popped a zit here earlier. Is it still bleeding?"

"Don't be a smart ass," said the officer.

Kurt stared at the officer in bewilderment. She shut the door and returned to the male officer, who had already knocked on the front door.

Mrs. Hitzges cracked the door and looked into the face of two police officers.

"Yes, can I help you?" she asked.

"We're sorry to bother you, ma'am," said the male officer. "Do you have a teenage son?"

Mrs. Hitzges' blood went cold. She was barely awake when she opened the door, but the mention of her son put her on high alert. He's upstairs asleep, she thought. Or was he? Was he out with John Paul? I've always known he'd get Kurt into trouble. "Yes," she said, "I have an eighteen-year-old son. Why?"

"Ma'am," said the male officer. "A car was stolen in Royce City. It was wrecked and abandoned about a mile and a half up the road from here in a ditch. We have a suspect in the patrol car. He doesn't seem to be bleeding, but we see blood here on the porch step. There may be multiple suspects. Someone is bleeding, probably from the crash. The suspect claims he was jogging. He claims his name is Kurt Hitzges and that he's your son. Is your son currently home?"

175

Kevin Cobb

Mrs. Hitzges' mind raced to catch up. The officers had thrown a lot of information at her and she was still trying to wake up. Sorting it out in her head, she understood that a car crashed into a ditch and hit Kurt while he was jogging, and that he was missing. She put her face in her hands and began to sob. "I told him not to run at night," she said. "This is exactly what I was afraid of."

"No, I don't think he was struck by a car. But someone's bleeding."

"Bleeding?" she repeated with alarm. "Is he okay?"

"Well, we don't know," said the male officer. "The blood doesn't appear to be coming from your son. We looked him over and it looks like—"

"Looked him over?" she interrupted. "You've' seen Kurt?"

"Yes, ma'am, he's in the cruiser. We—"

"He's in your car right now?" she asked,

"Yes, ma'am."

"And he's okay?"

"Oh, yes, ma'am, he's fine," said the female officer.

"What?" screamed Mrs. Hitzges, taking a step toward the cruiser. "He was here all along? You had me believing he was lying dead in a ditch! Why didn't you tell me he was in the car in the first place? I just lost my husband. I thought you were taking my son too."

"We're sorry, ma'am," said the male officer. "We were notified that a stolen car had been abandoned in the area and that the suspect had fled on foot. When we saw your son running across the lawn in a leather jacket we thought it was him. We apologize."

"We're very sorry, ma'am," repeated the female officer.

Mrs. Hitzges put her face in her hands again and shook her head. "Thank the Lord!" she said, then she stepped between the two officers, and descended the steps as quickly as her thick body would allow, on toward the police cruiser.

"Hold on, ma'am," said the female officer. "There may still be a suspect on the premises." She pointed to the bloody step.

Mrs. Hitzges scanned the step. "This is the blood you're worried about?" she asked. "No. That's Oscar's step."

"Who's Oscar?" asked the male officer.

"Our cat. When he kills rats, he drags them up here on the step so that we praise him. The step is always bloody. It looks like he's got a fresh one." Mrs. Hitzges turned and continued toward the patrol car.

The officers followed and released the mystified prisoner.

"We apologize, sir," said the female officer. It's hard to distinguish the farm boys from the bad guys."

"It's fine," said Kurt. "Next time I'll wear something sportier."

The male officer tipped his hat, and the officers climbed into the car. After a few minutes of paperwork the officers pulled out of the driveway. Kurt took a shower and went to bed.

Kevin Cobb

Chapter 18

The construction on Live Oak delayed Ranae's commute, and she needed a few minutes to find her assigned parking lot, but she still arrived at Good Samaritan Hospital at 7:22 a.m. She was due to report at 8:00. Determined to be on time for this all important first day of work, Ranae had allowed an hour and a half to reach downtown.

She was prepared, but the weight of beginning a career sat squarely on her shoulders. No more safety net. Ranae had always known Samson's was a safe and temporary stop, but she suddenly felt the inherent liability of being a registered nurse. Visions of med errors, malpractice suits, and revoked licenses crowded her thoughts. She needed to start her shift now and get it over with, but it was too early. Wasn't it? She closed her eyes and lamented the time she had frittered away waiting for exam results. Where had the time gone? Nothing but work from now on. She longed for just one more day without responsibility. She took a deep breath and slowly exhaled. She opened her eyes, gathered her purse, and opened the car door.

Wayne had started his shift half an hour before Ranae reached work. He had finished putting the bulk items away and began helping Junior enter a hefty pallet of repack. Junior scanned the barcode on a six pack of quarter inch O-rings and headed toward the red bin location requested by his scanner. "Do you ever question the Bible's inerrancy?" Wayne asked Junior.

"No," said Junior, as he reached into the repack box. "I used to, but I'm a long way from there now." Junior was a Ph.D. student at the seminary and had taken a few classes with Wayne. When Wayne first came to the seminary, Junior helped him land a job at Bailiff. "Why?" asked Junior. "Are you struggling?"

Junior turned left into the third aisle, placed the O-rings into one of the hundreds of small red bins, and scanned its location. "I don't know," said Wayne. "I guess I wonder from time to time. Don't you ever wonder if the

Bible we have is exactly what God intended? You've studied this stuff more than I have. You know the arbitrary process that produced the biblical manuscripts we use today. Aren't you afraid it's been corrupted?"

"Nah."

"Never? Why not?"

"Lots of reasons." Junior grabbed a bag of circuit breakers, scanned them, and began walking. "Well, first off, I wouldn't describe the process as arbitrary. In fact, that's one of the reasons I have for trusting the Word of God. God used all those early devoted Christians and all those monks over the centuries to transcribe the Word for us so that we have a faithful copy of scripture today. And the *arbitrary* you're referring to, guys like Constantine and Athanasius, right? The Council of Nicaea? I mean, that's what makes it so incredible. The process was so human, so many chances for it to be tainted, yet God perfectly used them to do his perfect work. Also, scripture was written over a period of hundreds of years by more than thirty authors. Not once did they contradict each other. That's impossible to account for without divine guidance."

Wayne cringed. He had hoped Junior could relate to his struggles. All through college and seminary, professors dodged sincere questions with pat answers they kept on the tips of their tongues. They could never just admit 'I don't know, it seems to be a contradiction' or 'I don't have a good answer for that.' Wayne's concerns weren't refuted with evidence or logic, but simply dismissed out of hand as liberal theology. Wayne reached into the repack box for another item.

"Also, there's the resurrection of Christ," continued Junior. "There's more historical evidence to prove the resurrection than the existence of Julius Cesar. Just look at the disciples. Almost all of them were martyred for proclaiming the resurrection. They were eye witnesses to the crucifixion. They knew the truth. If the resurrection was a fraud, the disciples would have known. In their hearts, they knew the truth and they all chose to die for their convictions. No one dies for something they know to be a lie. Right? So if the resurrection is proven, then the Bible must be true."

Wayne nodded in agreement as he carried another item down an aisle. I suppose it's reasonable, Wayne thought, but most of the historical evidence he speaks of comes from the Bible itself. Like Pascal's wager, it only works if I start with the assumption that the Bible is a reliable historical account.

Junior grabbed another item, but stood still in the middle of the aisle. "But that's not really what makes me believe," he said. "It's the things I've seen, the things I've experienced. When I pray, I feel God's presence. I've prayed for specific things and seen God provide in amazing ways. When God called me into the ministry, I balked because I knew I didn't have the money for seminary, but I prayed that if God wanted me to go to school, he would provide a way."

Junior looked at the item in his hand and walked slowly toward a red bin. "The very next morning," he continued. "Ron Bannister called me. He's a business man in my church back home. He told me God had laid it on his heart to pay for my schooling. I was shocked. I hadn't told anyone; heck, it had just happened the night before. No one

185

even knew I was considering seminary. Well, after that I never had any doubts. The disciples, the resurrection, the historical evidence, all of those exterior things are reassuring, but really, it's the evidence I've seen in my own life that makes me believe. I've witnessed too much evidence of God in my own life to believe scripture is flawed. Another time, my car broke down the day before I needed to drive my mom to the—"

An air horn screamed from the back of the warehouse. "That's probably UPS," said Wayne. "I'll get it." Wayne walked briskly toward the dock in the rear of the warehouse. He had experienced unexplained blessings as well. He also believed God had called him to the ministry through an odd progression of unexplainable circumstances and events.

The year following his calling, incredible signs of God's presence seemed to happen to him weekly. The summer before Wayne started at Vandyke, the transmission in his Honda developed a major leak. He needed $300 to repair it, but needed to save every dime just to make his school payment. That same week a church member handed

Wayne a check for $300. The church member told Wayne God had prompted him to donate to Wayne's schooling.

Wayne had always called these amazing events miracles until a systematic theology professor explained to him that a miracle happened when God temporarily set aside the laws of physics; multiplying fish and loaves, turning water into wine, and other inexplicable events that defy scientific explanation. Wayne's experiences weren't miracles, but God's providence. Wayne wondered if providence was another word for coincidence.

When Wayne reached the dock, a UPS driver tossed the last of several packages through the open dock door.

"What's up, my man?" said the driver.

"Hey," said Wayne. He dragged a flatbed cart to the dock and began loading the packages. The driver handed Wayne an electronic clipboard through the door. "Eight packages?" Wayne asked, as he signed the board.

"Yeah, eight," the driver confirmed.

"I heard we might get a little snow next week." Wayne handed the board back to the driver.

"You know I don't like that," said the driver, as he disappeared into the truck. "See y'all tomorrow."

"Have a good one."

Wayne moved the creaky cart toward the chest-high receiving desk. He opened each package and removed the shipping labels. As he entered shipping numbers into the shipping computer, his thoughts wandered back to his conversation with Junior. Those incredible events he had believed to be instrumental in shaping his faith had become shaded with doubt.

He remembered how his perception of God's daily presence used to direct his most pivotal decisions. Still, he couldn't comprehend how the creator of the universe could give mankind a divine message that needed to be defended with circular reasoning. God is Omnipotent, he thought. He's Omnipresent, He's Omniscient, yet he needs smoke and mirrors to reveal his plan to the world? Wayne finished entering item numbers and returned to the middle aisle. He picked up his scanner and quietly resumed helping Junior with repack.

Kevin Cobb

Chapter 19

Ranae approached the nurses' station, but the charge nurse was gone. She hated to ask for a translator, and she was embarrassed that she needed one. Instead of jogging, Gilmore Girls binges, or afternoon naps, she should have spent the past three weeks reviewing and sharpening her paltry grasp of Spanish. She had taken two years of Spanish in high school, but realized she hadn't retained any of it. In college, she had been advised to take Spanish, but believing she had retained enough to survive, she took four semesters of American Sign Language instead. She suddenly regretted the decision. Ranae searched most of the floor before finding the charge nurse in the south hall. "Brenda," she called out.

Brenda looked up at Ranae. "I'm going to have to give you twenty-three and twenty-four, too," said Brenda. "Sorry. Jim and April both called in."

Ranae looked at Brenda with a glazed over look. "No problem," she said.

Brenda continued hastily toward the nurses' station, then stopped and turned. "Are you ready for five rooms?" she asked.

"Sure," said Ranae. "I'll be fine. Also, I need a Spanish translator in room seven, please."

"I'll call it in," said Brenda. "And I'm requesting a PRN. If I can get one, she'll relieve you of twenty-three and four." Brenda turned and continued down the hall. "If you get too far behind, call me."

Five rooms? Ranae thought. I can't keep up with three, and twenty-three and twenty-four are on the opposite side of the floor. Ranae had been on her own for three days. The first two weeks on the floor had passed with ease. She followed an older nurse around, performing many of her responsibilities. Ranae had to learn a few details specific to Good Samaritan, but for the most part, the work resembled her clinical rotations; it was easy for two nurses to do the work of one.

When she was finally given three rooms of her own, her stress level skyrocketed. She knew charting was a big part of nursing, but it seemed to be endless. Whenever she started to chart, she was called to a room for pain medicine, or nausea, or to pass meds. Dealing with patients' family members was insufferable. When they weren't making requests, they were issuing demands.

The overload of responsibilities didn't bother Ranae, but she was disappointed with how little time she had for patient care. She became a nurse to assist and comfort people, but she struggled just to hand out meds, fulfill requests, and sprint to the next task. How would she manage five rooms?

"Hello, Mr. McDowell," said Ranae cheerfully, walking into room 1323. "I'm Ranae, I'll be your nurse today." After sanitizing her hands, she pulled a dry erase marker from her pocket and wrote her name on the white board on the wall directly at the foot of the patient's bed.

"Where's his pain medicine?" asked a large woman in the corner.

"Hello," said Ranae. "Are you Mr. McDowell's wife?"

"Where's his pain medicine? That last nurse promised she'd bring two hydrocodone an hour ago."

"Yes, ma'am. I'll go get him one. Let me check his chart and I'll—"

"You don't need to check nothing!" interrupted the woman. "He's been waiting an hour! Get him his pain medicine!"

"Mildred," said Mr. McDowell with a grimace. "Calm down. It's not that bad. I can wait a few more minutes."

"You're not going to wait *one* more minute!" said Mildred.

"I'll be right back with it, ma'am. Can I get you anything else, Mr. McDowell?"

"I'll be fine, honey," said Mr. McDowell with a pained but polite smile.

Ranae fulfilled the request and made her way to room 1324. Mary Evangeline was recovering from bypass surgery. She was timeworn, bitter, and silent. She refused to talk to Ranae or make eye contact. Although Mary's sour attitude had permanently worn a frown upon her once pristine face, she continued the meticulous maintenance of her long white hair. Ranae attempted to engage Mary in conversation, but was interrupted by the intrusive intercom. "Ranae," said Brenda. "Mr. Paultz is complaining of discomfort in eight."

"Thank you," said Ranae. "I'll be right there." Ranae faced Mary. "I'll be back in a few minutes with your meds, sweetie," Ranae said with a radiant smile. "After that we'll sit and chat. You have to tell me the secret to keeping your hair so beautiful."

Mary gave no response, gazing blankly at the ceiling. Ranae moved briskly down the hall, almost running to the other side of the nurses' station.

"Your meds are ready'" said Brenda as Ranae passed the desk.

"Okay, thanks." said Ranae. "Just give me a minute. Let me check room eight real quick."

Ranae entered room 1308. "Can I help you, Mr. Paultz?"

"Come here," Mr. Paultz whispered.

Ranae walked closer to the bed. "Yes, sir, what can I get you?" Mr. Paultz's eyes were closed, and he appeared to be in great distress. He whispered something in a muffled voice. Ranae leaned in close to hear. "What was that, sir?"

Mr. Paultz opened his eyes and reached for Ranae's chest. "Nice tits!" He said with a grin. Ranae slapped his hands away instinctively and ran from the room. She wanted to run to her car and cry, but she was too far behind to do anything but head for the nurses' station to begin passing meds.

Ranae was called back to Mr. McDowell's room as soon as she picked up her meds. She entered his room and was greeted once again by Mildred. "Where the hell have you been?" said Mildred. "Donavan needs more blankets, he's freezing!" Donavan had no blanket, only a hospital sheet, which inadequately covered his large frame.

Donavan was visibly trembling. He was curled in the fetal position, attempting to make himself as small as possible under the thin sheet. Ranae knew the floor was out of clean blankets and a delivery was past due. She held no ill will toward Mrs. McDowell. Donavan deserved better care, and Ranae hoped Wayne would advocate for her with the same ardor. The sight of Donavan broke her heart. He made eye contact with Ranae and attempted to apologize for his wife's aggression.

"It's okay," Donavan said. "I'm not that cold."

"Mr. McDowell, I'll be right back with some blankets. I promise." Ranae left the room amidst Mildred's verbal attack and ran to the nurses' station. "Are the blankets here yet?"

"No," said Brenda. "Hopefully in the next hour."

"What floor is the laundry done?"

"In the basement."

Ranae headed toward the elevator lobby. "I'm taking my lunch break now," she said. "I'll be right back."

"Ranae," Brenda protested. "You can't just go to lunch. You have to wait till you're relieved. Besides, it's only 9:30."

197

Ranae was in an elevator before Brenda finished talking. She stepped off in the basement, unsure where she was or what she was looking for. A long meandering hallway led her toward a poorly lit dead end. Before the tunnel halted, she passed a large door to the left; it was the entrance to a room that looked like an oversized laundromat. She ran past a long line of washing machines until she was standing in front of a long line of dryers. A man pulled several yellow blankets from a large dryer and put them into a large canvas cart.

"I need some blankets," said Ranae. "May I have two?" The man stared at her, confused. "I need two blankets," she repeated." Still, the man said nothing. Ranae reached into the bin and pulled out two blue blankets. They were so hot she could hardly hold the piping covers without screaming. "I need two of these, thank you." The man yelled at her in Spanish as she raced for the elevator. "I'm sorry!" she screamed. "Uh, *perdon, gracious*. Um, thank you!" On the elevator she cursed herself once again for her pitiful grasp of Spanish. This weekend, she thought, I'm getting Rosetta Stone.

Brenda confronted Ranae as soon as she reached the thirteenth floor. "Ranae, you can't just leave," said Brenda. "I'm probably going to have to write you up."

"I know Brenda, I'm so sorry. I just needed some blankets right away." Ranae entered Donavan's room without waiting for Brenda's response.

"I thought you'd never show up," said Mildred. "Donavan's freezing in here and you're off taking a smoke."

Ranae held one blanket under her arm while she covered Donavan from neck to toe with the other. He turned from his side to his back. "I'm sorry, Mr. McDowell," said Ranae. "I got held up." Ranae grabbed the second blanket and covered the bottom half of Donavan's body, tucking the remaining material snuggly under his feet.

"Ohhhh yeah," said Donavan. A peaceful smile enveloped his face as he peeked up at Ranae. "They're still warm. Thank you, honey."

Mildred continued her scathing criticism, but Donavan's smile confirmed to Ranae that she was born to be a nurse.

Chapter 20

The Friday following Kurt's brush with police, he met John Paul and Elio for a late snack at Tanoor Halal, a Mediterranean cafe.

"So I guess he crashed it over on Johnsville Road," said Kurt, "just a half mile from where it runs into 205. He must've gotten the hell out of there, because the cops never found him. By the time they were done trolling me he got away."

"That's just wrong," said John Paul, dipping his za'atar pita into cool ranch. "They can't just cuff you like that or force you into a cop car. That's practically abduction."

"It wasn't that bad," said Kurt. "I'd never seen the back of a police car before. It was kind of cool."

"Was it separated from the front with a window or a cage?" asked Elio.

"A window," said Kurt

"Did you piss yourself?" asked John Paul.

"No. I didn't know what was going on. I just knew I was innocent. Eventually they had to let me go."

"Dumb ass," said John Paul. "They could have framed you. They have to nail someone for it. They could have nailed you."

"Nah, I wasn't worried. There was no evidence against me."

"This isn't *Judge Judy*," said John Paul. "They don't need evidence. If a cop needs proof, he'll invent it."

Elio abruptly ended John Paul's rant by changing the subject. "I hit a skunk last week," said Elio.

"Where?" asked John Paul.

"On Dexham," said Elio. He grabbed the last chunk of his lamb kabobs. "I was driving to Walmart to get my mom some ice cream. I drove around the curve, that one by the big horse ranch, and right in front of me was two skunks. I would have hit them both, but I jerked to the right and just clipped the one."

"Does your car stink?"

"No, there's no guts on the tire."

"You're lucky. If you catch one on the undercarriage it stinks for a month."

"What was weird, though, is on the way home there were two dead skunks. I think the mate came back to mourn, then he got hit too."

"How do you know it was a boy skunk?" asked Kurt.

"I guess I don't."

"Maybe you hit both of them," said John Paul.

"No, when I hit the first one I saw the other one run into the bushes."

"Sad," said Kurt.

"That's a bitch," John Paul said sarcastically, looking at the menu. "Where's the waitress? I want some kanafeh. How's the marathon coming? You guys still running it?"

"For sure," said Elio. "I've been running since before Thanksgiving."

"Run with us," said Kurt, looking at John Paul. "It's not too late."

"No way," said John Paul. "I'm not running unless someone's chasing me. When is it, the sixteenth?"

"Yeah," said Kurt. "What's your time goal?" Kurt asked Elio.

"For the marathon?" asked Elio.

"Yeah."

"A time? I don't know. I'm just doing this for you. I'll be happy when it's over. I don't even know what a good time would be."

"Yeah, me neither."

Spectators sparsely lined the streets throughout the marathon route, but the crowd stacked up as Kurt neared the end. The twenty-sixth mile seemed like ten miles, but the twenty-six mile marker buoyed his spirit, and he could see the large blue arch marking the finish line.

Kurt attempted to sprint, but his body wouldn't respond. He recalled an Olympic marathon he'd seen on television as a kid. A runner from Ethiopia led the race as they neared the coliseum, but she had slowed to a jog. A Kenyan appeared on the horizon, closing the fifty yard gap between her and the Ethiopian.

The television coverage was hosted by two broadcasters. An announcer described the race while a former marathon competitor provided commentary. "Doesn't she see the Kenyan, Jim?" asked the announcer. "She needs to find another gear or she's going to get passed."

Jim laughed. "It's a Marathon, Ray. After twenty-six miles you are what you are. There is no other gear."

The announcer's wisdom landed fully on Kurt. There was no other gear. He knew his performance had fallen well short of his goal of finishing under three and a half hours. He had been confident three and a half would put him ahead of Elio.

Kurt seemed to finish second to Elio in everything. He was a superior athlete and always had any girl he wanted. His grades were always better. He was the all-district power forward while Kurt rode the end of the varsity bench. Elio's jewelry career had been planned for him by his father since his birth. Kurt's future was still clouded with ambiguity, but the marathon was supposed to be Kurt's day on top.

He had diligently trained for three and a half months, and he knew Elio had taken the race lightly, creating a rare opportunity to top him. Kurt wasn't interested in embarrassing Elio, nor did he plan on gloating. He just wanted a measure of mutual respect.

Elio and Kurt stuck together for the first five miles of the race, but Kurt couldn't maintain Elio's swift pace. Kurt hung back at a water station and told Elio, "I'll meet you at the finish line." Kurt expected Elio to weaken in the second half of the race, which would give Kurt a chance to run him down before the finish line, but Kurt never saw him after the sixth mile.

With less than a hundred yards to go, Kurt heard his mother's shrill voice shouting his name in encouragement. He glanced to the left for just a moment and spotted his mother and Monica. He ventured a second glance and saw Elio and John Paul standing next to his mother. Kurt had assumed Elio already finished, but he was disconcerted to see Elio already looking refreshed and relaxed. He was talking and laughing with John Paul and a thin brown-haired girl.

Was it Julie? They had texted occasionally since she had left for Florida, and she had texted him the day before the marathon to wish him luck, but she certainly wouldn't be here, would she? She wasn't due to get home till after midnight or the next day.

Kurt crossed the finish line as he read a giant digital screen displaying his time: 4:06. His head buzzed with conflicting emotions. He was relieved to be finished and disappointed to finish behind Elio, but Julie overrode all his concerns. Did she actually come home early to see him or was he just setting himself up for another disappointment?

Finishing the race turned out to be far less gratifying than he had imagined. Kurt hobbled away from the crowded finish line area with a water bottle in one hand and a banana in the other. His modest fan club made their way through the crowd to meet him. Mrs. Hitzges wrapped a thin blanket around Kurt and gave him a mother's hug. "I'm so proud of you!" she said. "I'm proud of both you boys." She fumbled through her oversized purse till she retrieved her phone. She made the boys stand together for a picture, then handed John Paul her phone and stood between them.

"How long ago did you finish?" Kurt asked Elio. "You had time to grab lunch and a shower."

"Nah," said Elio. "I haven't been done that long. I got here just before you did."

"Bullshit. What was your time?" asked Kurt.

"I don't know, I didn't look."

"Bullshit," said Kurt. "I know you saw it. A blind guy couldn't miss that screen. I'll see it online anyway; just tell me."

Elio looked at Kurt hesitantly. "3:27," he said.

"Damn, you suck," Kurt said, shaking his head with a smile and false disdain. "Nice job."

John Paul gave Kurt a bear hug. "Good job, bro!" he said.

"What are you doing here?" asked Kurt.

"I had to come see if you douches were going to go through with it."

"I didn't think you were coming?"

"Of course."

"Dude," said Elio, with a wide grin, "you owe me twenty bucks."

Kurt lost interest in the boy's conversation when he made eye contact with Julie in the back of the group, smiling brightly and waiting patiently to greet him.

Julie was tall and slender, with long, straight brown hair. Her petite chin and elegantly defined jaw line considerably softened her long aquiline nose. Julie moved to Rockwall from Houston in the middle of her eighth grade year, and sat by Kurt in her first period American history class. Kurt was the first person from the school to talk to her. By the end of the year they had become best friends.

Julie rushed in and gave Kurt a hug. He stiffened and pulled back, conscious of his own smell and filth. "Whoa," he said. "You don't want to hug me, I'm all sweaty."

"You just ran a marathon," said Julie. "I think that's normal."

They all turned and headed toward the distant parking lot. Kurt and Julie trailed the rest.

"What are you doing here?" asked Kurt. "How did you get here?"

"I came with your mom," said Julie. "She's been emailing me for weeks."

Kurt's heart dropped. She only came because Mom begged her, he thought. "You didn't have to come," he said. "It's no big deal really."

"You don't run a marathon every day. I wanted to be here. For you and Elio both."

Me and Elio both? Kurt thought. Just great. Kurt was embarrassed. He just wanted to go home, to be dead, to be anywhere but there.

"How did you get here already?" asked Kurt. "You weren't supposed to leave till this morning. Did you fly?"

"No. We left at two yesterday. Paulina was supposed to work last night, but she talked Wendy into taking her shift. We got in at 3:30 this morning."

"I can't believe you're here. Thanks for coming. You want to get some lunch this week or something?" Why the hell did I ask her that? he thought. She doesn't even want to be here.

"Duh." she replied. "I haven't seen you since August."

Her smile melted Kurt's chilled heart, and his courage revived. He recognized Julie's grey Acura in the parking lot and knew she had driven his mom and Monica because his mom hated driving in the city. After Kurt and Julie agreed on a Wednesday night dinner, the two boys continued walking toward Kurt's Jeep.

Kurt started the engine, but didn't want to move. His broken body was cooling off and stiffening. His feet burned like he had stood on hot coals, and his mind churned. She came to see me, he thought. She drove through the night, she even drove my mom and sister here. Maybe she sees me differently now. But Kurt's darker thoughts prevailed. Nothing has changed, he thought. To her I'm just a friend. She only came out of obligation. He turned to Elio. "Do you think Julie actually likes me?" he asked.

Elio stared at his phone, scrolling through Instagram posts. "She was happy to see you," he said. "I know that much."

"Do you think there's even a chance? Should I just move on?"

Elio set his phone on his knee. "Well," he said. "I could move on and John Paul could move on, but I don't think you can. I've known you forever, you get an idea in your head and you can't let go till it runs its course. Like this marathon. Now that we've finished this thing, I bet you won't run anymore. It's what you do. I think Julie drives you crazy because there's no resolution. No end. If she told you to get lost, you'd get over it in a couple weeks and move on. If you start dating, you guys might click, you might not. It's the ambiguity that keeps you coming back. I don't think you could ever just be friends with her. Ever. Maybe you should just tell her that. If she likes it, great. If not, then you can move on."

"I don't think I could do that."

"I'm not sure you could either, but it's the only way you'll break this cycle. It controls your life."

Elio was right, Kurt thought, but what can I do about it? I don't want to be just friends, but I also hate the idea of her out of my life forever. I simply have to win her over this Wednesday. "Do you think I'm a pushover?" he said. "Do you think she sees me as some desperate guy?"

"Don't listen to John Paul. He might get a few dates, but they all figure out pretty quickly that he's no prize. That's just not you, dude. You don't want to move from girl to girl to girl. So just keep it real."

"That's easy for you to say. If I were Elio Khoury, I'd love to keep it real."

"Kurt, you gotta quit talking like that. You're not a pushover. You're a gentleman. Girls like a gentleman. Julie likes a gentleman. That's why she likes you." Elio grabbed his phone and continued scrolling. Kurt drove on in agitated silence.

Chapter 21

Steve arrived in the OLA emergency room with a satisfactory heart rate, but his blood pressure had dropped to 86/52. After his blood pressure was stabilized, he was sent to the heart clinic. Within a few hours, his fatigue had dissipated and his breathing returned to the calm rattle he was familiar with. Dr. Dekker adjusted Steve's daily meds and sent him home.

Becca lived and worked in Uptown Dallas, twelve miles from Andy in Irving. Their turbulent childhood created a timeless connection they both valued and guarded. A week before Christmas, Becca met Andy at a privately owned coffee shop next to Becca's Pearl Street office.

"Mom said you've been stopping by Steve's house," Becca said.

Andy nodded guiltily. "Yeah," he said. "Every week or so."

Becca leaned in with intense curiosity and a sarcastic smile. "Why?"

"I don't know. He doesn't have anyone to check on him. He's all alone."

"He's all alone because he's an asshole. No one can stand five minutes with the jerk. He deserves to be alone."

"Yeah, I know."

"He's alone because he's chosen to be alone. He's so enamored with his own company he doesn't need anyone else."

"That's not true. He desperately wants company. He's just awful at dealing with people."

"To hell with him. You know he wrote me a letter a while back?" Andy glanced up from his iced caramel java with surprise. "What a joke," she continued. "He tried to give me a guilt trip. Said this may be my last chance to see my father. What an embarrassment." Becca took a bite of her egg and cheese croissant. "I figure I'll have to go to his funeral," she continued. "That's probably the last time I'll ever think of him. You'd be a lot happier if you did the same."

"He's our dad. What am I supposed to do?"

"Whoa, don't call him that. He's not our dad. He's our father, at best. He sired us, so to speak, but he's not a dad. A dad is someone who comes to your dance recitals, takes you on family vacations, is always in the living room watching TV and telling corny jokes. If you want a dad, call Jake dad. He's the closest thing to a daddy we'll ever have."

"Yeah, I know what you're saying, and I'm sure you're right. I just don't feel that way. Jake is great and I'll always respect him. I suppose I think of him as my dad as well. He's so great for Mom, but what if they break up like Dad— oh, sorry, I mean like our father and Miss Staley? If they break up, our relationship with Jake might vanish, too. There's nothing permanently connecting us"

"Vanish? Jake? Are you kidding? He's raised us since we were kids. *He* is our dad."

"He's better than a dad in some ways, but still, he's not my birth father. Jake has a special place in my life, but I only have one true father. Remember what it was like when Todd Bostic's dad died? He was shattered. He doesn't even have a dad now. Or a father. I bet he wishes his dad was alive, no matter how he treated him. Someday, maybe someday soon, I won't have a living father. When that day comes I'll wish I had one. So I choose to accept him as he is."

"As he is? After what he's put us through, put *you* through? I knew he was an asshole from the beginning. But you, you're so trusting. He broke your heart over and over again. I hate to think of you sticking yourself out there like that again. Todd Bostic was devastated because his father was amazing, ours wasn't and isn't. I'd rather have the memory of a dead respectable father than a living scumbag like ours." Becca picked up her phone. "I just can't do it, Andy," she said with waning interest. "Good luck." She took a sip of her non-dairy latte and lost herself in the world of hashtags, selfies, and food pics.

Chapter 22

As Kurt approached Julie's front step, the door opened and she stepped out. She wore jeans and a light brown jacket, her hair in a ponytail. It was the same look she usually went with, but Kurt recognized a transformation in her posture since leaving for Florida less than five months earlier. The meek, gangly girl he had chased through high school carried herself with a confidence and charm he had never seen in her. He always supposed Julie would fall for him eventually because he admired her in a way no one else appreciated. But his secret was out, her beauty was evident to anyone with eyes.

"Are you ready?" asked Kurt.

"Yep, where are we going?

"How about Casa Lupita?"

"Great! I haven't had good Mexican in forever."

Kurt reached to open the passenger door for Julie. She laughed nervously and waited awkwardly. After she got in, he shut her door and walked to the driver's side. Kurt had talked to her freely for five years, but he suddenly couldn't think of a thing to say. The lengthy silence was uncomfortable. Finally, Julie broke the ice. "How are you feeling? Sore?"

"Yeah, my feet are still pretty sore. And something hurts just below my knee. But I'm good overall. No doubt Elio is ready to climb Mt. Everest by now."

They both laughed, embellishing a weak joke to lighten the mood. It worked, and they soon returned to playful banter. Kurt talked about the tedious nature of his job at Maples Industry and John Paul's recent dating history. Julie talked about her least favorite classes and her roommate's peculiar eating habits.

"I'm taking a class at Eastfield in January," said Kurt.

"That's great!" said Julie.

"If my financial aid is approved I'll be able to transfer to UTD next fall. Meanwhile, I can get one or two of the basic classes out of the way."

"My dad loved UTD," said Julie. "He pressured me to go there, but I wanted to get out of the state. But next year I'm thinking of transferring to UTD. I kind of get homesick."

"Really? You might be at UTD?"

"I love FSU, but I miss home much more than I thought I would. Plus, it's so expensive."

"For sure! I love that idea."

"What you're doing is probably the best way to get through college. I kind of wish I had gone to community college for a year. FSU is too expensive. I'll be paying off student loans till I retire. To be honest, I only wanted to go there because of the beach. And I haven't made it to the beach yet. You're doing it the smart way."

The conversation progressed through dinner. The evening went as Kurt hoped until the bill arrived. Kurt grabbed the bill and looked for the total.

"How much was mine?" asked Julie.

"I got it."

"No. I can pay for my own."

Kurt's biggest fear was confirmed. She didn't view the evening as a date at all.

"Really, it's fine," protested Kurt. "It's no big deal. Anyway, this was my idea."

"My mom gave me spending money for the week," said Julie. "It's no big deal."

"Just let me pay for it," Kurt said with irritation in his voice.

"Well," said Julie as she laid a twenty on the table. "It's not my money anyway, so I'll just lay it right here. You can take it or leave it."

Kurt pulled money out of his wallet and combined it with Julie's twenty.

The two looked anywhere but at each other in awful silence.

"Are you ready to go?" Kurt finally asked.

"Yeah."

The ride home was cold. After ten minutes of silence, Julie glanced at Kurt sympathetically and produced a modest smile. She spoke in a slow, soft voice. "Hitz, we can't keep doing this. You're my closest friend, but we've been over this a thousand times. I just don't see you that way. Please, please, don't wreck this. I treasure our friendship."

A familiar emptiness came over Kurt, and the evening took a black tint. Julie was always within reach, yet totally unattainable. He could issue an ultimatum and force her to choose him as a friend or boyfriend, or he could acquiesce to her plead for the sake of preserving the friendship. His fear of losing her prevailed. "Yeah, you're right," said Kurt, mustering a positive countenance. "I get carried away sometimes."

Kurt squeezed Julie's arm, and they shared a polite smile. They managed to exchange small talk until they reached Julie's house. She reached across the console and gave Kurt an extended hug. Before she slid out of the Jeep she promised to stop by before returning to Florida.

Kevin Cobb

2018

Chapter 23

Steve was pleasantly surprised; several months had passed without another major setback. His physical decline was subtle, and yet a measurable drop in vitality and increase in fatigue from one month to the next was apparent. At school, the brutal honesty of youth was a constant reminder of Steve's looming demise. His students often pointed out the redness of his face when he exerted the least bit of energy, and they noted how gray his face was at rest. His loud breathing and wheezing also became a constant subject of conversation.

On a cloud-free day in late April, the Alexandria Panthers had an opportunity to clinch the district baseball title with a win over Tyler Heritage. The Panthers were ahead 7-0 by the bottom of the second inning.

Rick Piccipse, a lefty, was pitching for Alexandria with a runner on third base. The runner had taken a large lead off the bag. With his back to the runner, Rick began his wind up, but before he was set, the base runner sprinted down the baseline attempting a straight steal of home. Rick was caught off guard, but stepped toward home and threw the ball to the catcher, Jonathan Lane, who hastily stood in front of home plate, holding an outstretched glove. The throw arrived in plenty of time, but bounced wide and to the left. Jonathan lunged dramatically and the ball hit his glove, but fell to the ground. He picked up the ball and dove for the runner, who attempted to avoid the tag with a hook slide. In a close play, the runner was called safe.

Steve exploded out of the dugout and ran to home plate in protest. He ran on instinct, without considering his fragile heart. He hadn't run in over a year. His lungs demanded a surplus of oxygen his heart couldn't supply. When he reached home plate, he opened his mouth to confront the umpire but couldn't breathe. He bent over and grabbed his knees. A pained contortion gripped his bright red face.

"You okay pal?" the umpire asked.

Steve couldn't speak, but refused to withdraw his protest. He took his right hand off his knee to hold up his index finger, requesting a moment to catch his breath.

Coach Sturm and Frank Loxley stood helplessly by his side, and the infield walked cautiously toward the plate.

"He's got a heart condition," Jonathan told the umpire.

Coach Sturm looked Steve in the face. "Take a knee, Coach," said Coach Sturm. "Just breathe. Somebody bring him some water." He wrapped his arm around Steve's shoulder to support his weight; Frank followed suit, supporting his right arm. "Let's get you back to the bench," said Coach Sturm.

A freshman promptly scurried up to the coach with a Dixie cup of water.

As Coach Sturm took the cup, the Heritage third base coach interjected. "No, no," he said. "He doesn't need water; let's set him down here and let him catch his breath." The Heritage coach looked around for his closest player. "Call 911 and bring the AED."

Halfway between the on deck circle and the plate they lowered Steve onto the field in a sitting position. He rocked violently, still attempting to catch his breath as though he were drowning. Abruptly, Steve cringed violently and grabbed his chest as if he'd been shot; his chest jerked violently and his arms jumped, falling lifelessly to his side. Steve's defibrillator had been triggered by a dangerous heart rhythm. Steve let out a pained scream and went limp. The coaches kept Steve's air passage clear and continued to monitor his breathing until the ambulance arrived.

Chapter 24

The Bailiff warehouse was divided into four unequal quadrants by two broad perpendicular aisles. Each of the two aisles provided a wide enough berth for two forklifts or order pickers to comfortably pass side by side. The two quadrants nearest the office and storefront counter required the lion's share of the warehouse square footage and had two dozen narrow aisles, just wide enough for an order picker to safely navigate, used to store small to medium size items while the two rear quadrants were used to store bulk items.

Wayne loaded the orange order picker with the remainder of the bulk items and latched his harness onto the picker's safety lanyard. He drove halfway into a bulk aisle, and raised himself to the highest level. Anxiety rose in his stomach as he haltingly elevated beyond the daunting third level. He transferred the eighty-five pound box of floor sweep from the swaying picker onto the top shelf and scanned its location.

He lowered the picker and carefully navigated into a narrow aisle. He raised himself to the top level once again and unloaded five boxes of gloves. As he lowered the cab, his angst subsided. Before he could exit the aisle, Junior pulled in front of Wayne's picker on the forklift with a pallet of repack. Junior set the pallet in the middle of the aisle, adjacent to Wayne's picker. "I'm done with the bulk," said Wayne. "I can give you a hand."

Junior stepped off the forklift and turned to Wayne. "Alright," he said. "Are you ready for your Walton exam tomorrow?"

"Yeah," said Wayne. "I studied all week, but I'm hoping the essay question is only on antelapsarianism. If he asks about infralapsarianism, I'm dead. I didn't spend a half hour on it."

"Don't sweat it. It's simple. You already know this stuff; that's really what he talks about all semester. He wrote his dissertation on it." Junior stepped back onto the forklift. "I'll show you. Let me park this and I'll be right back."

Junior attempted to back up, but he had parked on a quarter inch seam in the concrete floor, preventing the unwieldy forklift from accelerating smoothly. He gave the forklift more throttle, jolting it free of the seam, sending the rear of the lift crashing into the base of the shelve frame beside Wayne's picker.

The upright beam bent and the large shelf leaned inward toward the forklift. The middle of the shelf protruded outward as the metal frame buckled. The massive shelf gave way and collapsed onto Wayne's aisle in a hulking wave of metal, cardboard, and dust. The shelf arched across the aisle and into the parallel shelf, causing it to cave in as well. The chain reaction toppled eight of the thirty foot shelves, burying the order picker and forklift alike in a sea of rubble.

When the collapse began, Wayne was standing in the cab of the picker entering numbers into the scanner. He heard a loud bang to his immediate right; as he turned his head, the entire world came down upon him. He was engulfed in a roar of unstoppable momentum. Although he ducked into the cab and covered his head with his hands, heavy debris from every side forced him flush against the Plexiglas windshield. A sharp pain pierced the back of his head as his world went dark.

A heavy brown dust suspended throughout the warehouse in an eerie moment of silence followed by a swarm of activity. Office employees and those on the counter poured into the warehouse led by Brian Ferguson, the warehouse supervisor. Customers at the front counter entered the scene of the astonishing catastrophe as well, horrified by the spectacular destruction and the humanity that surely lay beneath. Seeing the top of the forklift's mast, Brian climbed the jagged pile in a frantic search. He wildly grabbed boxes closest to the mast, casting them aside. "Come on!" shouted Brian, looking at the petrified spectators. "He's under here."

Soon after his hesitant colleagues joined in, a soft voice rose from the colossal mound of debris, but was too muffled to identify. The customers willingly joined the cause, but the rescuer's desperate efforts were constantly frustrated by the eroding sides of the hole they were digging. As they made progress, boxes toppled to the center. The circumference of the hole had to be continually expanded to keep it stable.

The voice grew stronger, and they could tell Junior was attempting to surface on his own. Sirens grew louder in the distance, and the amateur rescuers were buoyed by the promise of professional assistance. A trembling fist finally emerged from the pile. Brian grabbed Junior's hand firmly. "Hang in there, buddy," said Brian. "We got you. Just a few more minutes and you'll be out of there."

Two police officers entered the warehouse and hesitated, confounded by the terrible scene. One officer tapped his radio to apprise the fire department of the scene. The second officer ran to the focal point of the rescue. Junior emerged from the pile, shaken and bleeding from his ear. "Where's Wayne?" Junior asked.

"Wayne?" asked Brian. "He's under here, too?"

The rescuers' jubilance faded into confusion, followed by panic. "Where is he?" asked Brian, looking at a slow but steady stream of blood on the side of Junior's face. Brian pulled off his shirt and used it to stop the bleeding, attempting to lead Junior away from the scene.

"No. He's this way." Junior broke away from Brian and scrambled to the highest point of the rubble, desperately peeling back boxes where he thought Wayne's picker should be. Junior worked with his right arm only, his left dangling lifelessly at his side. One of the police officers followed Junior and directed everyone to join him. The mast of Wayne's picker was found quickly, and the rescuers moved to the spot. Loud, low pitched sirens approached, and within minutes four firemen took charge of the rescue. Three paramedics arrived as well. "Wayne!" Brian screamed. "Can you hear me?" Junior and Brian called Wayne's name repeatedly. An unspoken terror spread among the workers as they neared the eerily quiet picker.

When they finally reached the cab, Wayne was trapped, crumpled into the cab of the picker. He had a pulse, but was unconscious.

Chapter 25

Julie texted Kurt on her way back to Florida to apologize for leaving town without connecting again. She promised to see him at spring break.

Several weeks passed without contact. Kurt determined he wouldn't text Julie until she first texted him. Her birthday was in early February, creating a necessity to break the designed silence. He sent a brief text wishing a happy birthday and told her he was looking forward to seeing her at spring break. She didn't respond until eight o'clock that night, sending him a lone smiley face emoji.

Kurt felt like he had been punched in the stomach. Who the hell does she think she is ignoring me like that? he thought. All this anguish and contemplation over her, and all she's thinking about is her next exam. Why didn't I accept her rejection four years ago? I'd be long over her by now. I should be spending my time getting ready for college. There's lots of girls at UTD who will appreciate me. When I text them, they might even text me back.

He couldn't pretend apathy for long before he started to miss Julie. Giving up on her meant giving up on their lifetime friendship. He couldn't bear to do that. She'll come around in time, he thought. I just need to be patient. He stopped checking social media because it reminded him of Julie's absence.

Kurt rode these ever-shifting waves of emotion for the next two weeks with no sign of reprieve. In late February, he received a letter from UTD. He had been approved for enough financial aid to afford the fall semester. He was passing his Eastfield class with ease, and he spent most of his twelve-hour shifts on the dreary assembly line imagining his college experience. Teeming with optimism, he resolved to ignore all thoughts of Julie.

Kurt's confidence inflated whenever he hung out with Elio and John Paul. Their apathetic attitude toward girls was contagious. Even Elio expressed little concern with his girlfriend. He never seemed to worry about what she thought nor how she would react to his words or actions. If they broke up, he'd move on to the next one without regrets or anxiety. He lived for himself. So did

John Paul. Kurt envied them both and attempted to model his thinking after theirs. He was ready to move on.

In early March Kurt received a text from Julie:

Sorry I haven't texted. I've been so busy with school. I wanted to chat with you on my birthday, but had a paper due that day and an exam the next. It's been hectic ever since. I'm going to try my best to see you at spring break.

Kurt was instantly drawn back to Julie, but the familiar despair of chasing the wind returned as well. I can't keep falling back under her spell, he thought. She doesn't respect me. John Paul is right. If I want her, I need to appear indifferent.

He didn't respond to Julie's text for three days. Finally, unable to restrain himself, he sent a terse reply:

No problem

See ya then

As soon as he pushed the send button, a chill ran up his spine. He regretted sending the blunt reply. He contemplated chasing it with a more friendly text, but fought off the notion. He didn't talk to Julie or hear from her for the next week and a half. But spring break was less than a week away. He needed to communicate with her. She would be home, and his anticipation was rising. They needed to plan something before her family scheduled her entire week. His defenses crumbled once again:

> *When are you getting home? Do you want to visit UTD with me next week?*

Julie replied within ten minutes:

> *That would be great, but I won't be home for spring break. Sheila and Kelsy talked me into staying here. We've only been to the beach once this whole year so we're going to spend the week on the beach. Sorry. Let's do it this summer. I'm still considering UTD next fall. I applied last month.*

Kurt's optimism popped like a balloon. He pictured Julie laughing on the beach, tanning in her red and blue bikini, chatting with guys who were stronger, smarter, and more tan than he. He desperately resisted images of what she'd be doing at night. Kurt pushed through the disappointment and convinced himself that he didn't care.

Throughout March and all of April, Kurt battled conflicting emotions. He missed Julie and imagined what it would be like to see her every day at UTD, yet he was already embracing a Julie-free college experience, void of insecurity and rejection. By late April he was regaining his confidence and the resolve to turn the page on Julie.

The two exchanged texts sporadically in April, avoiding conversations about summer plans, but in early May Julie texted an invitation:

> *Ten more days! Can you believe it? Almost done with my first year of college. I'll be home on the eighteenth. We can get together that weekend if you're not busy.*

Kurt craved Julie's company, but he longed to be free of her mystical sway, to mature beyond his unwholesome dependence. The next morning he came to a conclusion. He would meet her, but this time he would call the shots. He wasn't going to rearrange his schedule or be inconvenienced. If she didn't make an effort to demonstrate interest on Saturday, he was through. He would turn the page with no regrets.

He responded:

> *I'm going to Monica's soccer game that Saturday. Want to come?*

Julie responded immediately:

> *Sure! Can't wait! See you soon*

Chapter 26

Steve woke up in the ambulance on the way to Our Lady of Angels. Andy was waiting tables when Coach Sturm texted him. Shortly after Andy arrived at the hospital, Dr. Dekker entered Steve's room.

"You had a big game today, huh?" Dr. Dekker asked. "Did you win?"

"I don't even know," said Steve.

"Well, you're fine now. Your ICD did its job. You got a little worked up and went into v-tach. It's common to lose consciousness. Some go unconscious before it's triggered, then wake up when it goes off. Others are conscious throughout. Your heart is back to a healthy rhythm, that's the important thing. The bottom line is, you're fine for now. However, your heart has declined significantly since the last time you were in the office. We're getting close to transplant time."

Dr. Dekker put his hands on Steve's ankles. They had swelled considerably since Steve's last visit. Steve took deep breaths as Dr. Dekker put his stethoscope on Steve's chest and moved it to various parts of his chest and back. The doctor stepped back from Steve and looked closely at his grey skin and jaundice eyes. "How's school been going?" asked the doctor.

"It's okay, the school year's nearly over."

"I mean your energy. How do you feel when you're teaching?"

"Well, that's not going so great right now. Tired, most of the time. I end up giving the students a lot of busy work because I don't have the energy to stand and lecture or even to keep them quiet while I'm teaching. I hope things get better when baseball is done."

Dr. Dekker looked at Steve in deep contemplation. "We don't want to wait too long. We want to get you on the list before your quality of life declines too far. Sometimes patients are miserable for months or years before they get on the list. We don't want to wait till you're too weak to walk or until you damage your kidneys. We have patients who get so weak their legs turn purple or even black. When they finally get a heart, they need months of physical therapy just to walk again. We don't want to wait that long. At some point teaching will become such a chore your life will become miserable. When you're too exhausted to work, when work becomes miserable all the time, it's time for a transplant."

"That's true right now," Andy interjected. "I know the thought of going back to school Monday is overwhelming to him. He sleeps in his recliner most nights because he's too tired to move to the bedroom."

Dr. Dekker turned from Andy back to Steve. "Is that true?" he asked.

Steve hesitated and looked at Andy with ambiguity, then back at Dr. Dekker. He shrugged. "Yeah. It's been a rough go lately."

"Let's do it then," said Dr. Dekker decisively. "We've prescribed all the drugs we can. You're nearly maxed out on Torsemide. If you're miserable, then it's time. Why wait? You can get it done now and be back to school by Thanksgiving."

Dr. Dekker left the room and returned a few minutes later with a nurse. He introduced Steve to Zoe, the transplant coordinator.

Zoe began the extensive process of placing Steve on the heart transplant list. Once a cardiologist recommends a heart transplant, the patient's insurance company is notified by the transplant coordinator for approval of the comprehensive testing necessary to determine if a patient qualifies for a heart transplant. Insurance approval usually comes through within five to ten business days.

Testing for heart transplant qualification is referred to as a "work-up," the umbrella phrase used to cover the extensive testing necessary to determine a patient's status as a potential heart recipient. A patient's heart is tested to determine if it is weak enough to justify replacing it with one of the limited number of available donor hearts. The patient's body is given a battery of tests to determine whether or not the patient's overall health is optimal to support a transplanted heart. Scheduling a work-up takes two to three weeks to coordinate because it consolidates dozens of tests into a two-day hospital stay.

A patient's status is usually determined before he or she leaves the hospital. If a patient qualifies for the transplant program, he or she goes home to await a second approval from the insurance company for a heart transplant. As soon as the insurance approval is received, the patient is placed on the UNOS transplant waiting list to receive a heart. The entire process takes six to eight weeks. In urgent cases, however, the entire process is often condensed into less than two days.

Kevin Cobb

Chapter 27

Steve waited impatiently for the insurance company to approve the work-up. Meanwhile, the baseball team was placed in the care of Frank Loxley and Coach Sturm. Steve knew he needed to get back to the classroom before he was replaced there as well.

After one day of teaching, however, he knew it was futile. He walked around his first period class passing out work sheets. It was the last time he stood up all day. He spent the afternoon fending off sleep. When the final class ended, he mustered the energy to walk across the building and into the head master's office.

On the drive home, Steve second-guessed his decision to take an indefinite leave of absence. He wondered if he would ever teach again. When he pulled into his driveway, Andy's blue Hyundai was parked on the street in front of the small ranch house. He entered the living room to find his son lounging on the couch watching television, a large blue suitcase at his side.

247

"Hey, Dad," Andy said. "Need a roommate?"

"What's wrong?" asked Steve. "Did you lose your apartment? Did you break up with Ashley?"

Andy laughed. "No," he said. "Most of my stuff is still there. I thought you might want some company for the next few months. I'd kind of like to keep my eye on you. We need to keep you in one piece till you get your new heart."

Steve looked at Andy's hulking suitcase, then back at Andy, wide-eyed and heart racing. Andy's offer disarmed him. "Well, sure," said Steve. "Yes. Of course. I'd never turn down my son's company."

Sharing a dwelling with any roommate is a challenge; Steve's stubbornness made it especially difficult on Andy. He signed up for as many extra shifts as the restaurant would give him, and he often stayed out late with Ashley, but most mornings and evenings were spent with Steve in the tiny living room watching television, playing poker, or arguing about sports. They struggled to establish an adult father-son relationship, but through trial and error the two figured out how to get along.

Although it was a difficult adjustment for Andy, Steve relished the opportunity to acquaint himself with the boy he never knew. He looked forward to knowing the man Andy had become. Whenever Andy was out, Steve walked as often and as long as he could, sometimes ten minutes, sometimes forty. Steve's trips to the Maverick Star became progressively sparse.

Steve looked up from his tablet to the scratching at the sliding glass door. The yellow mottled mutt looked back at Steve with hopeful anticipation. "Goddamn it," Steve said, straightening up the Lazy Boy to let Cornelius out into the back yard. Andy had brought his gentle dog to Steve's place while Ashley was on a two week business trip to San Francisco. Steve wanted to refuse, but acquiesced to keep Andy from leaving. While Andy was at work, the burden of pet care fell to Steve.

By the time Steve forgot Cornelius was in the back yard, he had returned, scratching at the glass once again. Cornelius bounded onto the couch as soon as Steve opened the door. "Get down!" yelled Steve, impatiently. The spirited mutt hopped down enthusiastically, circling at Steve's feet, awaiting the next command. Steve plopped on the recliner and seized the remote. Cornelius patiently sat at Steve's feet, watching him inquisitively, waiving his tail. Steve ignored him. Twenty minutes later, Cornelius was still sitting in front of him, poised for interaction. Steve looked at Cornelius with indignation. "Stupid dog," he said.

Whenever Steve put on his shoes, Cornelius dragged his leash to him, dropping it at his feet. Cornelius optimistically sat at attention, on his best behavior, trying desperately to make eye contact with Steve. "Go on, get out of the way," Steve would say, walking past him to the door. The leash hung on one of four coat hooks, four feet off the ground in the laundry room. Steve folded the leash in thirds and laid it along the top of the hooks.

Cornelius invariably managed to retrieve the hidden leash. When Steve put the leash in the garage, Cornelius sat at Steve's feet with the same piercing attentiveness. "What the hell kind of a dog are you anyway?" he said out loud. "You must have the blood of two hundred Goddamn breeds running through your veins." Cornelius jumped to his feet and approached Steve in anticipation, wagging his tail fervently. "Stupid dog," said Steve as he closed the door behind him.

Steve appreciated Andy's flexibility when it came to choosing a television program. Andy conceded control of the television to Steve, with one exception. Whenever Steve watched fishing shows, Andy quietly left the room. While Steve and Andy sat on the couch one evening, Steve made a point of asking Andy to watch a fishing program with him. Andy politely stood and left the room.

Andy's refusal to share Steve's hobby offended Steve's ego. One night Steve decided to express his frustrations. He knew Andy would be home for the night and a two-hour Bassmasters tournament would be on ESPN. An hour before Andy would be home, Steve drove to Bryant Avenue to pick up a Salami Picante pizza from Marzano's, Andy's favorite pizzeria. He would guilt Andy into watching a fishing show. Steve was convinced Andy would share his love of fishing shows if he just gave one a try. It might even lead to a day of fishing with his only son. Steve timed the pick-up so that Andy's beloved pizza would still be warm when he arrived.

Andy walked into Steve's living room and was hit with the familiar waft of Neapolitan pizza. "Is that Marzano's?" Andy asked curiously.

"Yep," Steve said with a proud smirk.

"Really?" asked Andy with suspicion. "Where did you get that?"

"I got it myself. It's still hot. I drove down there in the rain."

"Dad," said Andy, raising his voice. "You shouldn't have done that. Just ask me. I'll get anything you want."

"I didn't get it for me. I got it for you."

Andy's countenance softened. "Thanks, Dad," he said, reaching for the open box. "Don't do it again, old man."

"I promise." Steve changed the channel from the hockey game to the fishing tournament.

Andy's smile went flat. "Dad, I was going to watch that. Can you go back to the Stars game?"

"You don't care about hockey. Let's watch fishing tonight."

"They've got to win three of their last four games to make the playoffs. Turn it back."

"Nah, they suck. They won't win another game this season. I bought the pizza tonight. I get to choose the channel. Tonight it's fishing."

"Seriously? You're going to make me watch fishing on television? That's idiotic. If you want to fish, I'll drop you off at the park. I'm not watching fishing on TV."

"Just relax, one fishing show won't kill you."

Three bites into his first slice, Andy reached into the box with his free hand, pulled out a second slice, stood, and marched toward his bedroom. Cornelius bounced to his feet, eager to follow. "Thanks for the pizza, Dad."

"What the hell?" Steve protested. "I drive downtown in the rain, search ten minutes for parking, all out of breath. I bring you your favorite pizza and you won't even watch a goddamn fishing tournament with me?"

Andy turned around, "I didn't ask for pizza. You never should have driven down there. You're in no shape to be running around in the rain."

"Well, go on then," said Steve in a pout. "Go on to your room."

Andy stood in deliberation. After a long sigh he returned to his spot on the couch. The two ate in silence. When the pizza disappeared, Andy pulled his phone out and ignored both Steve and the television. Steve's anger turned to curiosity. What disturbed Andy about a fishing show? Steve wondered. Andy wasn't offended by anything else I did. Why did fishing raise his ire?

Not wanting to offend Andy further, Steve spoke gently. "I'm sorry, son." I had no idea you hated to watch fishing so much." I'd love to *take* you fishing, but I can't get my boat out anymore. I get too tired. I thought we could do the next best thing and watch it on television. Fishing is the most father-son thing to do, right?" Steve laughed nervously.

Andy's bitter face turned away in disgust. The silence irritated Steve. "Fine," Steve said angrily. "We'll watch something else." He turned the channel back to hockey. The Stars game had finished and the postgame show was on. "You should try fishing before you despise it," Steve continued. "You always hated fishing just to spite me."

Andy's bottom lip quivered. "Do you know the name of my fishing camp?" asked Andy with a faltering voice. Steve stared blankly at Andy, unsure what his question meant. "Do you even remember that I went to fishing camp?" continued Andy.

In the back of Steve's mind he struggled to retrieve a vague memory of Veronica mentioning Andy attending a summer camp, but Steve had no recollection of it being a fishing camp. "Yes," said Steve, unconvincingly. "I know you went to camp."

Kevin Cobb

"Fishing. The only positive thing mom ever said about you is that you loved to fish. My dad, the one I saw about three times before I was six." Andy's voice was still shaky. "I ignored all the negatives she told me about you and clung to the image of a great fisherman. When you finally showed up I was in awe. You were a hero, a super hero. I didn't know anything about fishing, but I was sure that you would teach me. You bought me a fishing pole for Christmas and a little tackle box for my birthday, but you never once took me fishing. We lived two miles from a lake. I asked and asked and asked. But you always said next time. Shame on Mom for covering for you! She should have told me from the beginning that you couldn't be trusted, but even after that, you got my hopes up again, telling me you'd take me to Lake Fork, just you and me. Three times you promised and stood me up. Finally, one day out of the blue you took me to the lake. I was so excited. You showed me how to cast a spinning reel and we caught five bass. It was the best day of my life. Until we got back to the dock and you told me that you were leaving Texas and moving to North Carolina."

Andy paused, walked to the lounge chair facing the couch, and sat. Cornelius sat and looked sideways at Andy. Fire raged in Andy's eyes as he penetrated his father with a stare. Steve sat in stunned silence, unarmed and tongue tied.

"Really?" Andy said, his voice no longer meek, but commanding. "You take your kid fishing for the first time to tell him that you're going to abandon him. Again?" Andy paused and looked at the ground. "But you know what? Even after that I still wanted to impress you. I still wanted your attention. I still wanted to learn to be a fisherman so you'd want to spend time with me." Andy looked at Steve again. "I asked Mom once, I only had to ask her once, Dad, if I could get fishing lessons. Mom found a camp in Forney, Camp King Fisher. She sent me there for a whole week, then one day a week for the rest of the summer. Most of the kids at camp had a dad or brothers or at least an uncle to fish with. Whenever I talked to you on the phone I asked you to come visit me so I could fish with you. Don't you remember us talking about this on the phone? The weekend Mom flew me to North Carolina

257

to visit you was the weekend of the new Harry Potter movie. All I wanted was to see the movie; it would have only taken a few hours. Instead, I sat alone in your apartment an entire Saturday while you were at a fishing tournament."

"Andy," Steve interrupted. "I wasn't myself back then. I didn't want to fish that tournament. A friend signed us up without telling—"

"I'm not done, Dad," Andy said, silencing Steve. "When you moved back to town we finally started to hang out. You took me to baseball games, out for ice cream, movies. And I loved that. We didn't see each other often, but when we did, it was fun. You lured me into your trust again, and I fell for it all over again. We planned that fishing trip to Saskatchewan. We were supposed to fly in on a seaplane, rent a boat, and stay in a log cabin. I couldn't wait. I had never been out of the country. I've *still* never been out of the country. But mostly, we were going to be alone together for five days, and I was going to learn to fish with my dad. I waited on the porch with my suitcase for an hour and a half before Mom told me your truck broke down on the way. The trip was cancelled. I was sad because I wanted to go, but mostly because I didn't want you to feel guilty for letting me down. That Sunday Becca came into my room and showed me a Facebook post. Her friend, Jennifer Meeks had liked a post that her father was tagged in, Jeremy Meeks."

Steve's heart dropped at the mention of Jeremy Meeks.

Andy continued. "He was at Tazin Lake, Saskatchewan with three other guys holding fish. One of those guys was *you*. You preferred fishing with your buddies over your own son. Andy stood. "I'm here for the long haul, Dad. I'll hang out with you, I'll mow your yard, take you to appointments. I'll wipe your ass when it comes to that, whatever you need. You're going to get a new heart, and I'll be so happy for you, but I don't want anything to do with fishing." Andy turned and walked to his bedroom followed closely by Cornelius.

Steve sat frozen on the couch with his elbows on his knees and his face in his hands. The pungent smell of pizza sauce still lingered in the air. "Nice job Steve," he said out loud. "Real mature." He wished he could redo the entire evening.

He searched his memory for a phone conversation with Andy about fishing camp, but couldn't bring anything to mind. I was so caught up in my own life, he thought. I couldn't even give my son the best part of me. I've alienated myself from everyone who has ever loved me, and I have no one to blame but myself.

For the first time in his life, he caught a glimpse of self-awareness. He understood the candid truth of who he was. Goddamn it, he thought. I'm an asshole. I'm nothing but a self-centered prick.

Chapter 28

The cardiac output test determined whether Steve's hospital stay would end or if he would be admitted for a work-up. He was taken into the cath lab to evaluate his heart function. The nurse left Steve alone in the cold quiet room, shaking under a thin blanket, his arms shivering against his sides. He wanted to protest the delay, but he was sick of acting like a jerk. Instead, he stewed in silence.

Fifteen minutes passed and the nurse hadn't returned. Why can't they put me to sleep? he thought. Wake me up when it's over. Who the hell does this doctor think he is? I'm naked and freezing here while he's out sipping cocktails on the golf course. Steve closed his eyes, took a deep breath, and exhaled slowly. Alright, pull yourself together, Steve. When they come back, I'm nice and calm. Just get through this.

At long last he heard muffled chatter in the adjacent room. A door opened, and the room filled with activity. A lanky woman in a mask and hair net stood in his line of vision. "My name is Cindy; I'll be your nurse for this procedure. How are you doing, honey?" she asked. Steve looked at her but said nothing. "We're about to get started," she said.

Steve nodded to her in silence. After Cindy walked away, a man with a dark complexion wearing a surgical mask and glasses stood in Steve's vision. "Good morning, I'm Dr. Umrani. I'll be doing your heart cath this morning." The doctor disappeared from Steve's line of vision, and Steve could hear him talking to the staff and preparing instruments behind the head of the bed.

"Alright, Mr. Dunham," said the doctor. "I'm going to begin by numbing your neck with some lidocaine. You'll feel a stick."

Steve involuntarily tightened his body in anticipation of the poke. His neck was jabbed by a short needle. The doctor applied pressure to the syringe, pushing the lidocaine into his neck. Dr. Umrani's breath reverberated in Steve's ear and he could smell the doctor's amber and lavender cologne. The needle was removed, then pierced his neck again a centimeter to the left. By the time he'd been pricked four times, the medicine took affect and the pain tapered off.

"All done. Are you okay, Mr. Dunham?"

What the hell does he want me to say? Steve thought. Don't be a jerk, Steve. Be nice. "Yeah," he said.

"Okay, let me know if this hurts."

A warm liquid ran down Steve's shoulder, and he knew his jugular had been pierced. He closed his eyes and bit down hard. The pain was only vaguely present, but he couldn't ignore the unnerving pressure of a large metal object being forced into his neck.

"Are you still okay?" asked Dr. Umrani.

Steve nodded, trying to ignore the large needle protruding from his neck, but the word *jugular* sat heavy on his mind. He only heard the word in mob movies and sports metaphors as a symbol of death. Having various staff members inspecting and probing his bleeding jugular made his skin crawl. He was exposed and at the mercy of strangers.

"Okay, Mr. Dunham, the worst part is almost over. You'll feel some pressure, then the hard part will be done. Are you still Okay?"

Steve subtly nodded. Stop asking me that, he thought. Just get it over with.

Dull but persistent pressure compressed his throat, restricting his breathing and temporarily cutting through the lidocaine. As the pressure was applied, Steve held his breath and grunted through the discomfort, but the final jab induced a verbal yelp as he arched his back off the table.

"Sorry, Mr. Dunham, but the worst part is over now; the starter is in. The rest of the procedure is easy."

Steve took comfort, but the sense of vulnerability persisted. The guide wire stung lightly as it was threaded through his veins and into his chest.

"Are you doing okay?"

No response.

The doctor studied a monitor and discussed his observations with the staff. Steve closed his eyes and desperately tried to visualize the lake, fishing on a picturesque day, reeling in a hulking bass.

"Still doing okay, Mr. Dunham?"

"Yes!" Steve responded violently. "I'm fine, damn it! Quit asking. Just get it the hell over with and quit talking to me."

"I'm sorry, Mr. Dunham," said Dr. Umrani calmly. "It's uncomfortable, I know. I'm sorry, but you're all done. The procedure is finished. We'll get you out of here real soon. Your cardiac output is at 1.8. You qualify for a heart work-up." Dr. Umrani looked at Cindy. "Put him on a milrinone drip and find him a room." Steve was taken for a chest x-ray, then admitted onto the heart floor.

Steve lay on his back motionless, looking to the left, as he had in the cath lab. The swan catheter remained in his neck to deliver milrinone to his failing heart. The nurses attempted to persuade Steve to move his neck freely, but the bulky dressing and pressure on his neck made him apprehensive about moving his neck. He reflected upon his outburst in the lab. Damn, he thought. Why am I so intent on being a horse's ass?

Someone's hand covered his own, and Andy appeared in his line of vision sitting in a chair to the left of the bed.

"Hi, Dad," said Andy. "How do you feel?"

"I'm fine. I'll be glad when this is over."

"Does your neck hurt? It's okay to move it."

"Yeah, I know. I just don't want to."

"No rush. Maybe this afternoon."

Steve closed his eyes and fell asleep.

Two hours later a nurse rushed into Steve's hectic room to stick his arm and collect thirty-two vials of blood. Another nurse entered with a single needle that plunged deep into Steve's wrist in search of an artery. He responded with a loud scream and a protracted torrent of swearing. Later that evening, a male nurse with a polka dot hair net came into Steve's room to place a peripherally inserted central catheter, also called a PICC line, in Steve's arm and remove the swan. Steve refused to allow the PICC line to be inserted.

Andy had stepped out after Steve's multiple blood draws to grab a bite to eat. When Andy returned to the floor, the charge pulled him aside just before he re-entered Steve's room. After a short conversation, Andy went in to talk to Steve. His neck moved freely and he turned to greet Andy.

"What's going on with this PICC line, Dad?" asked Andy. "The nurse told me you wouldn't let them put it in."

"I don't need it. They want to tether me to a pump twenty-four hours a day. No way. I don't need it."

"When you start getting this medicine, you're going to have so much more energy."

"Who's complaining? I don't need more energy. I'm still walking an hour a day."

"An hour? Really? More like ten minutes, twenty tops."

"I'm still walking. That's what counts."

"For sure, Dad. It's great that you're still active, but you need this. It's the first step toward a transplant.

"No. They want to run a tube from my elbow through my body to my chest. I don't think so. I'm not talking about this anymore, Goddamn it! Leave me alone." Steve rolled over and closed his eyes. He lay broken on the hospital bed, sore, tired, and hungry. While he feigned sleep, he cursed himself once again for being a jerk.

Later that afternoon, Dr. Dekker walked into the room and sat to the left of Steve's bed.

"Steve," Dr. Dekker said.

The familiar voice immediately grabbed Steve's attention.

"What's the problem?" asked Dr. Dekker. "They tell me you won't let them place a PICC line. You can't get your milrinone delivered without it. Your energy will improve significantly once you've been on milrinone for a few days. But it's only effective if you're receiving it continuously. So you have to let them place a PICC line."

"I don't need it," said Steve. "I walk an hour every day. Walking around tethered to that thing will only slow me down. No matter how much energy it gives me, it'll prevent me from getting out and staying active. It's not worth it."

Dr. Dekker leaned in closer to Steve. "Let me explain the importance of the milrinone more clearly," he said. "There are three status levels on the transplant list. One-A, is emergent. This is for patients with a heart so debilitated they're hospitalized and in need of a transplant right away. Thank God, you're nowhere near this yet. The next is One-B. This is for someone who is living at home and attached to a milrinone pump. They are second priority after One-A. Patients who are Two-A need a transplant, but are living at home and are not on a milrinone pump. Right now you'd be Two-A. When we put you on milrinone, you'll be One-B and pushed up the list significantly."

A light bulb illuminated over Steve's head. "Oh," Steve said. "So I need it to get a heart sooner?"

"Precisely."

269

"Oh. Well, okay then. Why the hell didn't someone just say that in the first place?"

"That's what we've been trying to tell you," said Andy.

Dr. Dekker smiled. "You just weren't ready to hear it yet." He patted Steve on the arm and briskly left the room.

A half hour later, the nurse with the polka dot hair net returned and inserted Steve's PICC line. He made a small painful incision between Steve's right biceps and triceps. The nurse inserted almost two feet of medical tubing, snaking it through his body. An x-ray confirmed the tube was correctly positioned in his chest, and the incision was sutured tight around the tubing, anchoring it to his arm.

The remaining tests and procedures were non-invasive. Steve was wheeled all over the hospital for various tests and screenings and often returned to his room to find medical personnel waiting to take him to yet another test.

Zoe explained to Steve that donors are paired according to three basic criteria. The first is blood type. Steve had O+ blood, simple to match. The second criteria pertains to antibodies. A donor and recipient cannot carry the same antibody. This didn't apply to Steve because he carried no antibodies. The third criteria is the donor's heart size in relationship to the recipient's. A donor's body may be larger or smaller than the recipient, but their heart size must be relatively similar.

That night Steve couldn't sleep. He wanted to talk to Andy, but they hadn't exchanged meaningful words since their fishing confrontation. He knew a contrite apology was the necessary first step toward becoming a decent person. He turned to Andy across the room, looking down at his phone.

"Son," said Steve. "I really need to talk to you."

Andy stood from the threadbare futon and walked to Steve's bedside. He sat on the chair to Steve's left. "Sure, Dad," he said. "What do you need?"

271

Steve's confidence was dashed as they made eye contact. "You should go down to the cafeteria and get something else to eat," said Steve. "You've got to be hungry, and you look so bored sitting around here."

"That's what you had to talk to me about? That I can go get something to eat?"

"Yeah, I know you won't go unless I tell you to."

Andy looked at Steve quizzically. "What is it, Dad?" asked Andy. "What's really wrong?"

Given a second chance, Steve still couldn't produce an apology. "I haven't gotten out in my boat in months," he said. "I don't think I ever will. Afterwards, you be sure to go get the boat and my fishing gear. If you don't want it, you can sell it. I don't mind. I don't have much to leave you, but I've got that. I'm sure Becca doesn't want it."

"Don't talk like that. You're not dying. You're about to get a new heart. Things aren't getting worse; they're about to get better. Much better." Andy's shifting eyes couldn't convince Steve that he believed his own counsel.

"You heard Dr. Dekker," said Steve. "They've never done a transplant on a transposed heart patient. The plan is to cut me open, put me on bypass, and only then figure out how to make it work in less than four hours. That's not exactly a confidence boost. I'm pretty sure this is it for me."

"That's ridiculous, Dad. Dr. Dekker was confident your surgery would succeed. Plus, he wouldn't have brought you this far if he wasn't confident they could pull it off."

"No," Steve said, staring theatrically at the ground. "I'm going to die. I know it." He looked up and realized he had upset Andy. Steve put on a smile. "But who knows, many a slipped twixt a cup and a lip."

"What does that mean? Twixt a cup and a lip? You've said that since I was a kid and I've never understood it. I've never heard that phrase anywhere else."

Steve laughed. "It's from an eighties movie, *Young Guns.* I don't usually like westerns, and there weren't a lot of westerns being made in the eighties. But I loved *Young Guns*. It's a movie about Billy the Kid."

"Really?" said Andy with disappointment. "You got it from a movie?"

"So, Billy and his gang were cornered and they had no way of escaping New Mexico. Charlie, one of his pals, was freaking out because he saw a bulletin that announced their gang would all be hanged if they were caught. So Charlie asked Billy to reassure him that they weren't going to hang. The whole gang looked to Billy for comfort. Billy looked Charlie dead in the eye and said, 'Well, Charlie, if we get caught, we're gonna hang.' His gang didn't like that answer at all. Then Billy laughed and said, 'But many a slipped twixt a cup and a lip.'"

"That's it? That doesn't explain anything."

"Sure it does. If you have a can of beer in your hand and you look down at that Coors light, you know that beer is going to end up in your belly. Nothing can stop it; it's a forgone conclusion. But how often do you see a guy take too big a gulp and spill it all over his shirt? Or you're too drunk and you drop the whole can. Or you set the beer on the ground and some dumb ass kicks it over. The beer escaped your mouth against all logic. Many a slipped twixt a cup and a lip."

Andy laughed and shook his head. "Sorry, I asked."

"Don't you get it? It means even when all hope is gone, you never know when the tables will turn in your favor and you end up victorious. Like in last year's Super bowl. The Falcons were crushing the Patriots by four touchdowns. Everybody assumed it was a blow out. But somehow, the patriots won. Many a slip twixt a cup and a lip."

"Okay Dad, if that helps you, great, but this is no long shot for you. You'll be fine."

Steve knew he had already delayed his apology too long, but the busy day and a multitude of new medications had drained him. Since he could barely keep his eyes open, he yielded to the night and fell asleep.

By late Thursday morning, the heart clinic had collected enough data to evaluate Steve's physical condition. Ninety-one revealing test results demonstrated that Steve's heart was sufficiently deficient, yet his overall health was adequate to justify receiving a rare and priceless heart. The heart board approved Steve, and the final hurdle was to obtain a second approval from the insurance company, this time for a transplant.

Zoe Contacted Steve's insurance company and expected to receive approval within the day. She brought Steve a contract, a written commitment between hospital and patient. Steve promised to obey all hospital and heart board regulations during the time between leaving the hospital and the transplant surgery. He wasn't permitted to drink, smoke, or use unauthorized drugs. He wasn't permitted to stray beyond fifty miles of the hospital. Before he left the hospital, a nurse disconnected his PICC line from the IV pole and connected it to a portable milrinone pump. The pump was placed inside a small duffle bag about the size of a football. Andy pulled his car to the front of the hospital and drove Steve home.

Steve arrived home without hearing from the clinic. He was too nervous to relax, so he climbed into his truck, and searched the messy cab for a stable place to hold the tethered pump while he drove. He was afraid to balance the cumbersome pump bag on his lap. If it tumbled onto the floor, the tube could pull out, risking infection. He finally settled on the console, closing the top compartment on the bag's shoulder strap. This secured the pump, but the scant length of tubing restricted his motion and kept him from having full range to turn the wheel with both hands, so he mostly steered with his left hand.

He drove to the lake and muddled along the rocky shore. The high summer clouds moved lazily across the horizon, and the early evening heat made him drowsy. He sat on a bench and watched three boats under the bridge. They were surely crappie fisherman hoping to find a school in the cool and shaded depths. A lone boat trolled along the opposite shore, beating the banks for black bass. The world moved steadily along without him.

Steve's phone rang. "Hello?" he said.

"Mr. Dunham?" said Zoe. "Your approval came through."

Steve's heart jumped. "Really? Just like that?"

"As of 5:00 p.m. You'll officially be on the UNOS heart transplant list. Congratulations! Make sure you have your phone on and charged at all times. From the time you're called, you'll have ten minutes to respond before the heart is offered to the next patient on the list."

By the time Steve walked back to the truck, the clock read 5:03. Steve's excitement turned to anxiety. A call could come in any minute. A thousand risk factors and unnerving scenarios invaded his mind.

Andy's fishing tirade left a poignant impression on Steve, and he became increasingly aware of how he was perceived by others. He had made a concerted effort to be polite in the hospital, but failed at the first sign of discomfort. He remembered the self-absorbed letter of desperation he'd sent to Becca and realized his words had been harsh. Maybe he could still make peace with his daughter. As soon as he returned from the lake, he pulled out his yellow legal pad to write her once again:

Becca, I miss you. I know I haven't been the ideal father. You deserved better. But time is short, and I want to see you again. I am on the heart list. I could receive a heart any minute. How the surgery goes, no one can say, but I really want to see you before then. I beg you to respond and hopefully to come see me. It is my dying wish.

Make an old man happy and pay me a visit.

Dad

When Becca received Steve's letter, she opened it out of utter curiosity. The last letter she had received from him was so smug and arrogant. She wanted to see if he could possibly outdo himself in inept parenting.

The melancholy tone of the letter surprised her. It still reverberated with hubris, but he was beyond the delusion that a meeting would be a favor to her. He was openly asking, even begging, for a final visit. She had no

Kevin Cobb

intention of responding, but was amused by his change in tactics.

Steve sent a similar letter to Becca each of the next three weeks. She disposed of each one unopened.

Chapter 29

Julie was sitting on the top step of her spacious front porch when Kurt pulled into her driveway. She stood and approached Kurt's Jeep.

"Didn't the game start at four?" Julie asked, looking at Kurt through the passenger window.

"Yeah," Kurt said without putting the gear shift into park. "We're only twenty-five minutes late. Besides, it's U8 soccer, not the world cup."

Julie opened the door and jumped in. She reached across to hug Kurt. He leaned toward her, but kept his hands on the steering wheel. Julie patted his back awkwardly and sat back in the passenger seat.

"What's the name of Monica's team?" asked Julie.

"The Pink Lightning."

"Cool! I was on the Cheetah Girls when I was seven. I don't think we ever won a game. But I scored three goals that year. Only two of them counted, though. The other one was in the wrong goal."

Julie laughed. Kurt gave her a token smile without taking his eyes off the road. Julie's laugh tapered off into tense silence. After several uncomfortable moments she continued. "I played defense mostly." Denied a response once again, Julie looked blankly out the passenger window.

Kurt knew he had overplayed his indifference. He hadn't planned on being rude; he was aiming for self-confident independence, someone used to attention. "Sorry I didn't stop by sooner," said Kurt. "I wanted to come see you when you got in last night, but Kendell Monroe came over to study. She's in my Algebra class, she needed a study partner."

"That's great!" she said. "There's about ten of us in Dr. Picard's Western Civ class who get together the night before tests. Luckily, it's a co-ed dorm so we can cram all night. When is your test?"

"Thursday."

"Are you ready for it?"

"Yeah."

"Oh," said Julie. "I almost forgot! I received my acceptance letter from UTD in March. I still don't know if I'm going back to FSU or not."

"Yeah?" Kurt mumbled coldly.

"The lady I talked to at UTD said all my classes would transfer. I wouldn't lose anything."

Kurt's heart lightened. He was afraid his face had given him away, but he reigned in his emotions and maintained indifference.

"Hmm," Kurt murmured.

Julie's joyous countenance crinkled into a concerned scowl. "What's wrong, Hitz?"

"Nothing."

Julie remained quiet for several minutes. Kurt turned onto St. Andrews toward the soccer fields.

"It's no fun going to a soccer game if you're going to be grumpy," Julie said. "What's your problem?"

"We don't have to go to the game."

"I didn't say that. I just want you to act like yourself. Why did you invite me to a game if you're going to be a jerk? Talk to me. What's wrong?"

"Nothing. What do you want to talk about?"

Julie shook her head in silence. Hoping to end the unraveling conversation, Kurt turned the radio up. Julie turned it down immediately. "Take me home," she said, then she turned the volume louder than before. She fixed her eyes out the passenger window. Kurt pulled into the next driveway and turned around. No words were spoken on the return trip to Julie's house. She stormed out of the Jeep without saying a word and closed her front door without looking back.

Kurt pulled away in shock. What happened? he thought. How did this happen again? Is it over, just like that?

His best friend was gone and he didn't know how to respond. Anger? Vengeance? Relief? As he vacillated between emotions, the familiar loneliness covered him like a blanket. As he neared home, he knew he wasn't ready to turn in for the night. He couldn't face a long evening of mental anguish alone, and he didn't want to face his mom, who would ask about Julie and question why they missed the game. He pulled to the side of the country road and texted Elio and John Paul to meet him at Studebaker's.

John Paul responded with a yes. Elio responded just before Kurt turned onto Smith Street. Kurt pulled over once again to read the text. Elio was in Dallas with his latest girlfriend; he wouldn't make it. A half mile after Kurt pulled onto FM-552 his rear view mirror was filled with a mystic teal Toyota Corolla.

A few seconds later John Paul pulled alongside Kurt to pass. Kurt usually yielded to John Paul's shenanigans, but today Kurt was imbued with unbridled aggression. He glanced at the forty-five MPH sign and accelerated, preventing John Paul from completing the pass. John Paul was surprised and intoxicated by Kurt's sudden moxie. He punched the accelerator to match Kurt's surge. The two cars approached eighty miles an hour on the narrow country road.

An oncoming vehicle suddenly appeared on the horizon, a hundred yards in front of them. Both boys instantaneously stopped accelerating, keeping them side by side. Kurt instinctively hit the brakes to allow John Paul to pull in front, but John Paul thought the same thing, hitting his brakes as well. As the oncoming car grew larger, the two friends looked at each other across the solid yellow line in full panic. Just before the honking Chevy reached them, John Paul jumped on the accelerator and pulled in front of Kurt. The Chevy passed safely to the left.

John Paul was giddy when they reached Studebaker's. Kurt was frantic. "That was bad ass!" said John Paul. "Can you believe we didn't die?"

"We're so stupid," said Kurt. "What the hell were we thinking?"

"That was great! I looked over at you and thought you were gonna shit yourself."

"We almost died," said Kurt.

"It makes you happy to be alive, though, don't it?"

John Paul was right. The few seconds of panicky hesitation and adrenaline overload were exhilarating.

A waitress led the two boys to a table in the back corner, next to a large rectangular window. The waitress laid two tattered menus on the small square table and left them.

"You know," said Kurt. "Your 'I'm the prize' thing doesn't work."

"Whatta you mean?"

"I just threw it down on Julie and it blew up in my face."

John Paul laughed. "Really? You tried it? You probably did it wrong."

"No. I was cold and indifferent, like you said. I never backed down. She wasn't impressed. She was pissed."

"What a douche. I didn't tell you to be a prick. It's a subtle attitude, not a boycott."

"Whatever."

Kurt unloaded his heart break on John Paul for the next hour. They left the restaurant to find a hookah bar in Dallas.

"I'm drinking tonight," said John Paul. "You better drive."

"Where are you going to get alcohol?"

"People think I'm forty."

"Are you kidding? You always say that, but you're, like, five foot tall. It never works."

John Paul laughed. "It always works," he said. "You should grow a beard. The beard is power."

They took Kurt's Jeep downtown and shared a pineapple with an ice tip at Three Pyramids hookah bar. John Paul's beer request was denied. After twenty minutes of puffing, Kurt's head throbbed.

He stopped smoking and drank some herbal tea. His head cleared up and he soon lost himself in conversation about Julie. Hashing out his relationship issues with John Paul gave him a new perspective on Julie. Their relationship consisted of Kurt chasing and Julie running.

Lots of chasing, lots of running. Chasing sucks, he thought. I need to let the game come to me. Just be young and have fun. John Paul never frets about tomorrow or yesterday. He just soaks in the moment. That's all I need to do.

John Paul persuaded Kurt to drive to his uncle's gas station in Mesquite, another eastern suburb, where he was sure they could get beer. They exited the interstate and drove south on Lawson, another two lane country road. The night was starless and cloudy. The city lights tapered as they entered the wooded countryside and was replaced with total darkness. A lone vehicle drove fifty feet ahead of them.

"Warp him," said John Paul.

"What?" asked Kurt.

"Warp him. That car in front of us," said John Paul, pointing to the brown sedan directly ahead.

"What does that mean?"

"When it's this dark, you turn off your headlights and drive right up on their bumper. Then, when you're right up on their ass, you turn on your lights and flash your brights. They can't see you in the mirror with your lights off. Then you scare the shit out of them. You warp them. It freaks them out, scares the hell out of em."

"No way, they might wreck."

"Nah, it just pisses them off. My Cousin, Akeem, does it all the time."

Kurt had followed conventional wisdom his whole life, and it had gotten him nothing but a vanilla lifestyle, safe and boring. "What the hell?" said Kurt, with a devilish grin. He shut off the headlights and accelerated.

John Paul whooped and nodded in triumphant support. "Hell yeah!" he said. "Hitz is a bad ass!"

Kurt closed the gap quickly. "Now!" screamed John Paul.

Kurt flipped on his high beams. The Chevy swerved violently into the northbound lane. The driver over-corrected, veering the skidding car back through the southbound lane and into a drainage ditch, where it abruptly stopped.

"Oh shit!" yelled John Paul.

"What the hell?" said Kurt. "They're off the road." Kurt slowed to a crawl and saw that the car was undamaged. The stunned driver sat still and the lone passenger was swearing at them and making hand gestures, but no one was hurt.

"I've never seen anyone freak out that bad. Drive!"

"Should we stop?"

"Drive! Make a U-turn and jump back on I-80. It's just ahead. Get on and head back to Dallas."

A mile and a half down the road, Kurt jumped onto I-80 and headed west toward Dallas.

"They're gonna call the cops," said Kurt.

"You better drive all the way to Dallas. We'll take the back roads home."

Kurt weaved through sparse traffic topping eighty-five miles per hour. He feared jail and wondered what it would do to his college dreams. Immediately after the I-80/

I-30 merge the rearview mirror was filled again, this time with blue and red flashing lights. "Oh shit," said John Paul. "Here we go again." Kurt pulled onto the shoulder and turned off the ignition.

Chapter 30

Steve abruptly sat up in bed at 8:32 a.m. He franticly checked his phone, but there were no notifications, no call from the heart clinic. He thought about his stay in the hospital, snapping at the doctor in the cath lab and again at Andy about the PICC line. I'm still a jerk, he thought. It doesn't matter how hard I try to change. I'm a jerk. How does a forty-eight-year-old stop being a jerk? What's the first step?

Steve untangled himself from his tubing and retrieved the pump hanging from the headboard. He showered, took his morning meds, and walked into the living room. Cornelius greeted Steve with a cheerful wag of his tail, but Steve lumbered past him and into the kitchen.

Steve grabbed a hard-boiled egg from the refrigerator, set it on a napkin, and sprinkled it with salt and pepper. He opened the fridge again and grabbed a piece of honey ham. He laid the ham beside the egg, grabbed both, and sat in the recliner. Cornelius sat patiently in front of

Steve while he ate. "You don't give up, do you?" said Steve. Cornelius's ears raised. Steve tore a small piece off the ham and threw it at Cornelius. The dog swallowed it in one ferocious bite. Steve finished eating and drove to the heart clinic for a regularly scheduled appointment.

The waiting room was crowded, but Steve found a seat directly across from two older men. One was in his early seventies and wore a surgical mask. The other was a decade younger. He was overweight and wore denim overalls.

"I got a letter from my donor's family last month," said the man in the mask. "He was a plumber, so his truck was full of dozens of conduit posts, those twelve foot rods. He was driving in the rain, slid off the road, and hit a telephone pole solid. The conduit come right through his rear window and, well, ya know, it must've been pretty awful."

"Plumber shish kabob," said the man in the overalls. He laughed and looked around for a reaction. "You know, I never found out who my donor was. I never wanted to know." He laughed and looked over at Steve's milrinone bag. "It makes sex that much more fun," he continued. "Every time I have sex I'm having a threesome. I just don't know if it's two girls and a guy or two guys and a girl."

The man in the mask stood in disgust and walked to the other side of the waiting room. Steve remained quietly retrospective, seeing himself mirrored in this obtuse stranger. Gratuitous banter no longer appealed to Steve. If he wanted to stop acting like a jerk he had to avoid blathering with people like this. He had to stop *being* someone like this. He knew a reprimand would be the height of hypocrisy, so he sat in silence.

The man in the overalls looked at Steve. "Don't worry, partner," he said, "you'll get to use that thing again. You got a noodle now, but once you get that new heart you'll get your fire hose back."

If Steve had been paying attention he would have been offended to the point of cursing, but he was distracted by something he saw in the hallway through the glass door. A tall black gentleman had gotten off the elevator and was pushing a walker toward the clinic door. The man looked twice the size of the others in the hallway, like a man among toddlers.

The nine foot clinic entrance seemed pressed to the limit as he walked through and into the waiting room. The man's presence brought with it a mysterious air of celebrity or novelty that quieted the room and caught everyone's eye.

He was the tallest man Steve had ever seen. He had a broad chest, yet he was trim. Steve guessed he was a bit older than himself, but still ten years younger than anyone else in the waiting room.

After the man laboriously pushed his walker into the middle of the waiting room, he paused to take several deep breaths. The mountainous man had a small duffle bag slung over his shoulder. Medical tubing ran from the bag to his arm.

The tall man found a seat behind a coffee table, four seats to the right of Steve. His knees jutted out from under the table like an adult riding a small tricycle. Steve wanted to inquire of the man's height, but refrained. The new Steve isn't going to ask rude questions, he thought.

Everyone in the room looked at the giant, but only the man in the overalls spoke. "You must be ten foot tall," he said.

The tall man smiled. "Actually," he said meekly, "Seven, five."

"Goddamn," said the man in the overalls. "Where do you get your clothes?"

"Everything is custom made. Nothing off the rack for me. See this walker?" The tall man pointed to the walker, standing nearly four and a half feet off the ground. "I had to get this custom made."

"Are you getting a new heart?"

"Lord willing," the tall man said with a gleeful laugh. "I sure could use it, but King Jesus knows what I need. He's never let me down yet. I've been at this for a long time. I've walked out of hospice twice. One time my heart function was at six percent. They've tried to bury me a few times." The tall man paused to chuckle. "But King Jesus just isn't ready for me yet."

"Well, hell," said the man in the overalls. "You're bigger than life. If anyone deserves a heart, it's you."

"Oh no," said the tall man. "I get by. I have no complaints."

"You sure have a rosy attitude. I was an old man when I needed a new heart and I was still pissed."

"The good Lord wakes me up faithfully every day. He's done it for fifty-one years. How can I complain? My son Jeffery developed leukemia when he was just twelve years old. He fought hard, but that chemo just stole his strength. He lost his hair. He was so thirsty. Always thirsty. In the end he was put on a breathing machine. He was hurting and he was tired, but he never complained. He never asked 'why me, Daddy?' He never cursed God. He just endured the trials, and King Jesus rewarded him by taking all that pain away."

The room was silent and uncomfortable. He grinned. "But God is good," he said. "I reckon I have nothing to complain about. If God has a heart for me, I'm ready. If not, then Jeffery is waiting for me in the Kingdom."

A nurse entered the waiting room. "Devin Keith," she announced.

The giant took a deep breath, put his hands on his knees, and stood. He joyfully looked into the eyes of the man with the overalls. "It was a pleasure talking with you sir," he said.

"You, too," the man in the overalls replied.

Devin made eye contact with Steve and they shared a gentle smile. He greeted the nurse, ducked his head and shoulders under the doorway, and disappeared into the office.

Steve racked his brain trying to remember a basketball star named Devin Keith. Surely he'd been a basketball star on some level. He pulled out his phone and googled, Devin Keith, expecting to find pictures of a star basketball player, possibly even a former NBA star, but he found nothing. He googled "7'5 Devin Keith" and "7 foot Devin Keith." He tried different spellings and various possibilities, but found nothing.

Steve was perplexed. Even if Devin was an uncoordinated beanpole, Steve thought, he was tall enough to reach the highest levels of basketball, and Devin was no beanpole. His physique resembled Magic Johnson's, except that Devin was eight inches taller.

That night, Steve sat in the recliner to put on his walking shoes. Cornelius sat in front of him and resumed his fervent tail wag. Steve looked down and made eye contact with the mutt. "Why do you keep following me? I'm an ass. You know that first-hand." Cornelius's ears perked up, and he stood to meet Steve's attention.

Steve's stubbornness crumbled before the boundless enthusiasm of the patient mutt. Steve walked into the garage to retrieve Cornelius's leash. "Can you teach me to be a human?" asked Steve. As he connected the leash to the triumphant dog's collar, Cornelius licked Steve's face, tickling his ear. Steve pulled back in surprise, but smiled. "Can you teach me to live grateful?" He stood and they walked to the door. Cornelius gained a walking partner, Steve gained a friend.

Steve walked Cornelius down Balleywood Avenue, across East Sixth Street, and into the Catholic cemetery. The sun had disappeared, but the June heat remained. Still, Steve preferred it to the day time, and he slept too late to take advantage of the relatively cooler mornings. His small reservoir of energy was declining daily, but he still appreciated the thrill of working his dwindling heart.

Steve's thoughts returned to Devin Keith. Who was he? Steve wondered. He apparently made no mark on the sports world. A man with his charisma and inimitable physical attributes could have ruled the world if he just had a healthy heart, yet he carried himself with pure joy and gratitude. His son was taken from him so quickly, yet he wasn't bitter or angry. He may have been the kindest man I've ever met. He must have had those questions thrown at him ten times a day, every day of his life. How many times had he been asked how tall he was? Nevertheless, he answered patiently and respectfully, like he was hearing the question for the first time. He was patient and totally unselfish. He was *unselfish*. That was it, Steve thought. That's the difference between Devin and me. I'm completely absorbed with the petty matters of my own little world. Devin is totally unselfish. He's concerned with everyone except himself.

The evening heat wore on Steve, and he knew he didn't have the strength to walk to the far side of the cemetery. Cornelius loved exploring the neighborhood, but was panting and ready to retreat to the air conditioning as well. Steve pivoted and headed toward home.

I'm selfish, Steve thought. That's it. That's my problem. I'm going to continue to be a jerk as long as I'm self-absorbed. I'm not selfish because I'm a jerk. I'm a jerk because I'm wholly selfish. I've never invested in anyone my whole life.

He surveyed his life, his friendships, and his relationships. When I married Veronica, I never considered what I could bring to the table for her benefit. I never thought about how I could make her happy nor how I could make her life better. I only thought of how she could please *me*. She would have done anything for me. She'd still be with me if I hadn't left her. But I was an awful husband because I was a self-absorbed prick. I'm an awful father. I'm a bad co-worker. I've never been a good friend.

He had been oblivious to the fatal flaw in his character his entire life, but it suddenly stood out like a second nose. Breaking this life-long pattern of jerky behavior isn't a mystery, he thought. I've got to learn to be unselfish, consider someone else for a change. A ray of light illuminated Steve's heart, and he believed he had taken a significant step.

As he exited the cemetery's stone gate, a despairing thought occurred to Steve. He knew that heart size could not be accurately measured by body size. Still, Steve couldn't imagine a donor existed with a heart big enough to replace Devin's.

Steve crossed Sixth Street and began the long trek up the gradual ascent. His phone rang. It was Our Lady of Angels.

"Hello?" said Steve.

"Is this Mr. Dunham?" a female voice asked.

"Yes,"

"Hi, Mr. Dunham," she said with excitement. "This is Zoe. We found you a heart."

He had expected a long tedious wait. Time to reflect on life and put things in order. He'd only been on the list six days. Zoe told him to check into the hospital by 12:30 a.m. He walked as fast as possible, eager to get home to Andy. His heart rate soared as he considered the vast possibilities awaiting him. When he reached home, Andy was gone and his phone went to voicemail. Steve left a text message and drove himself to the hospital.

Chapter 31

Wayne was roused by the fresh air soon after he was pulled from the tattered warehouse. He woke up lethargic and confused. After paramedics stabilized his injuries he was loaded into an ambulance and rushed to Parkland Hospital. He'd been struck on the back of the head by the corner of a box containing a thirty pound industrial motor, causing a subdural hematoma. The injury kept him in the hospital for four days. Additionally, he suffered a bruised kidney and a broken right humorous bone. His arm was set in a cast from his elbow to his knuckles. The doctor restricted him from physical labor for a minimum of six weeks. Besides, the warehouse would take more than a month to repair.

Ranae insisted that he quit his job at Bailiff. He stayed away from the warehouse for the time being, but knew he couldn't quit. Instead, he spent this unplanned sabbatical creating a résumé in anticipation of his upcoming graduation. Upon the completion of his thesis and final summer class he'd be ready to enter a pastorate and leave the warehouse life behind forever.

Wayne did his best to capitalize on his time off. He sent résumés to fifty churches throughout the country. After three weeks, he had received just five responses, each to inform him the position had been filled.

He hadn't solved his lingering doubt issues and refused to think about his theological angst. Whenever he allowed himself to ponder the spiritual, he was invaded by the conviction that the colossal warehouse accident was God's chastisement for his life of hypocrisy. All Christians, whether Calvinistic or Arminian, fear divine punishment when living a lie because a person's natural sense of justice prevents him or her from believing that a bad deed can go unpunished.

He forced his doubts into a small box in the depths of his mind and shut the lid. He placed all of his theology, philosophy, and faith qualms into the same box, refusing to think of divine matters at all. The modicum of faith he preserved only served to convince him God was angry. This frightened him so deeply he refused to ponder the divine ramifications.

After he exhausted all possible résumé avenues, Wayne slid into the doldrums of idleness. He passed his rehab time by playing Madden 12 on his X-Box 360. He hadn't played the outdated game since college, but the mind-numbing repetition brought him a measure of comfort. This attempt to pass the time became his full time occupation.

He had always stressed over his school work and refused to hand in assignments until every detail was perfect, but the overachieving flame had been extinguished. Since the accident, he accomplished only the bare minimum to get his assignments in on time. Weeks passed without a visit to Walbrook.

On the Friday of Independence Day weekend, Ranae sat beside Wayne on the couch, watching him lead the Cowboys to another Madden championship. "Take me out," she said. "I wanna go somewhere."

"Huh?" said Wayne.

"Let's go out. I can't watch you sit around like this anymore. Let's go do something. Take me out."

"You know I can't take you out. I'm not supposed to be driving yet."

"Fine," said Ranae. "I'll take *you* out. Where do you want to go?"

"How about right here on the couch? Let's have a Madden tournament."

"No. We're getting out of this apartment. Do you want to choose or do you want me to?"

"How about a movie? A new Vin Diesel movie is coming out this week."

Ranae disappeared into the bedroom, and Wayne lost himself in the video game.

Ten minutes later, Ranae emerged from the bedroom with a suitcase. She dramatically flung it onto the living room floor, then disappeared into Wayne's office. Wayne's curiosity pulled his attention away from the electronic football game, and he watched the office door for Ranae's next appearance. Instead, he heard a loud crash in the office. He gingerly shuffled into the tiny office to find Ranae on her hands and knees in the closet tugging on a large object. Within a few seconds she dragged out their blue waterproof tent. Ranae turned to Wayne. "We're going camping. I'm getting you away from everything. No X-Box, no movies, nothing. Just me and you."

"Camping?" he said. "It's awfully hot for camping, and I won't be much help building a campsite."

Ranae turned to him with a disgusted glare. "You don't think I can put up a tent?"

Wayne smiled in deference with his hands in the air. "I think you can do anything." Awakened from his stupor, Wayne was taken aback. Ranae was working full-time while nurturing him back to health. He was acting like a baby, and she was proactively boycotting his pity party. His guilt rebuked him for forcing her to be the bad guy.

Ranae located the rest of the camping equipment while Wayne packed their suitcase. A wine cork on the back of his dresser caught his eye. The sentimental cork hadn't entered his mind since the day Ranae gave it to him. Where had the time gone? He had assumed they would have exchanged the cork several times by now, but school, résumés, and his chronic skepticism had consumed his time and cluttered his mind.

The cork needed to be kept in a more visible spot. He carried the small suitcase to the car with his good arm, dropped it into the trunk, and set the cork in the driver side cup holder. Hopefully, the cork would remind him to plan a special date the next time he brought coffee to the car. Ranae finished securing the camping equipment and drove the two of them to Purtis Creek State Park, an hour southwest of Dallas.

At the wooded campsite, Wayne dragged a few dead tree branches to the concrete fire ring with his good arm and sat on a lawn chair to watch his wife pitch the tent.

"It's ninety-five degrees out here," said Ranae. "I don't know why we need a fire."

"It's not camping without a fire. Besides, I feel bad enough watching you do everything. A fire gives me something to do."

Ranae finished pitching the small tent and sat next to Wayne. He handed her a cold Dr. Pepper. They ate turkey sandwiches and cubed cantaloupe out of a plastic container. Wayne ate a half a bag of sourdough pretzels.

When they finished eating, they walked to the modest size lake and onto an L-shaped dock. The sun eased into the horizon. A father fished from the dock with his three young children. He scrambled between the children, struggling to keep their hooks baited and their lines untangled. A cormorant dove below the surface of the calm lake and reappeared twenty feet to the left. After a quick look around, it dove again. They watched the last vestiges of the sun disappear below the thick green trees on the far side of the lake and returned to their campsite.

An hour later, brilliant stars illuminated the black sky. Wayne took a chocolate bar from the cooler, unwrapped it, and divided it into eight unequal pieces. Ranae pulled a sleeve of graham crackers from the bag and handed half a cracker to Wayne. He put a chocolate into his mouth, took another with a graham cracker, and placed it on the stone closest to the fire. After breaking the limbs off a thin tree branch, he shoved two marshmallows onto the end and hung it over glowing orange coals.

"Put one on for me," Ranae said, handing him another half of a graham cracker. "But don't put it right on the stone. That's gross."

Wayne put the cracker and a piece of chocolate on the aluminum foil paper that came with the chocolate and placed it on the stone.

Wayne looked at Ranae. "Thank you, Rabbit," he said.

"For what?"

"For this," Wayne said, looking around the campsite. "For everything. For bringing us here, for setting up the campsite. Even if you did pitch the tent on a bump." He said playfully.

"On a bump?" she said in protest. "I don't think so, babe. And you've got to admit, you've never put up a tent that fast. I kicked your ass in tent setup."

Wayne laughed again. "You kicked my *ass*? I don't think I've ever heard you cuss before.

"It made you laugh. I'm going to swear more often."

"It's tough to have a pity party when *you're* around," he said. "You keep me on my toes, and you make me smile. When I'm pouting, you kick me in the *ass*."

Ranae smiled. "Of course. That's what we do, right?" she said. "I love you."

"I apologize for moping all month."

"You had a horrific accident. It'll take time. Just relax. Don't worry so much."

"Yeah, it's time to pull myself together. Time to move on."

Ranae pointed to Wayne's marshmallow; it had caught fire. Wayne angled the stick from the fire to his mouth to blow on the marshmallow. Wayne laughed. "You've always got my back."

Late into the night, Wayne woke up with a crushing headache. His concussion symptoms had diminished, but his headaches persisted. He slipped out of the tent and walked to the car. He opened the glove compartment and found a bottle of Advil.

The half-moon glowed amidst the starlit sky. He Leaned against an ash tree and looked back at his unwashed car and the lake beyond. The tops of the pines danced with a steady breeze that brought a welcome relief from the heat. He looked at the two green bumper stickers on the front of his Honda and sighed dramatically as he read:

I Think, Therefore I'm Vegan

I wish I had such strong convictions about *anything*, Wayne thought.

He walked back to the lake and returned to the L-shaped dock. He sat with his feet dangling off the edge and looked across the dark water and flooded timber rising from the lake. Like most Texas reservoirs, Purtis Creek had been impounded by the Army Corps of Engineers over thirty years ago. They left the large pines behind to drown. The dead trees stood smugly in the lake as a defiant and haunting forest. The wind blew harder, stirring the choppy water. The barren trees creaked and moaned in the wind.

Wayne welcomed the stiff breeze, but he continued to sweat. Blurry memories of a crashing warehouse and the echoes of a deafening collapse compounded his headache. A bright star sat just below the moon, and he wondered if it was Mars or Venus.

His mind reluctantly returned to theology. He considered God and hell, St. Justin, and Bishop Butler. He considered Bonhoeffer, Pascal, and Goethe. The loud lapping water reflected a fuzzy version of the moonlight. From every direction, the aggressive song of the cicadas seemed to scold him; Rheee! Rheee! Rheee! Rheee! Rheee! Nature expressed anger with him, and a wave of indictment climbed his spine.

Despite his monumental doubt, Wayne knew he wasn't right with the creator. Evidence of the designer interrogated him from every angle. God's creatures were staring at him accusatively. Wayne's skepticism splintered, replaced by the unpleasant awareness that he was at odds with the God he had known and trusted since his childhood. He had run away from a steadfast rock in search of stability on a desolate and shifty beach. The Bible had always given him sufficient answers until he had made the decision that it didn't.

He stood and walked briskly to the car, overwhelmed with the desire to understand God afresh. He usually kept a Bible in the car, but he could only find a water-stained paperback edition of the Gospel of John, left behind from a summer class.

Wayne opened to the first chapter and started reading. He didn't know what to look for, but trusted God to throw him a life preserver. Halfway through Chapter Six he came to the Bread of Life discourse.

Jesus spoke to a crowd, claiming to be the Bread of Life, saying that no one can approach the Father except through the Son. Many in the crowd found his teachings confusing, arrogant, and possibly cannibalistic. Verse sixty-six grabbed Wayne's attention; 'Many of his followers turned back and no longer followed him.' Jesus turned to his twelve disciples and asked, 'You do not want to leave me, too, do you?' No, thought Wayne. I don't want to leave. He had read this passage dozens of times, but had never personalized it. He read the next verse with hopeful anticipation.

'Simeon Peter answered Him, 'Lord, to whom shall we go? You have the words of eternal life.''

Wayne surveyed the vast diamond spotted sky. Yes, he thought. Where else would I go? It's one thing to stop believing in Jesus or the Bible or the Church, but where does that leave me? I can't make myself believe the world exists without a purpose. I'm not an atheist. Discarding my faith leaves a void that I can't possibly leave empty. It would be more difficult for me to believe in nothing than to believe in Christ.

"Lord, to whom shall we go?" he repeated out loud to the open lake. Between Christ and nothing, he thought, I must choose Christ. Christ is the only game in town. "Only You have the words of eternal life," he said. "Only You."

Wayne's headache had receded, and he was ensconced in a familiar peace he hadn't experienced in years. He knew he was ignoring the most basic rules of Bible interpretation. The verse was intended as a description of a historical story, not as a prescription for life principles. Professor Lance would tell him that he had taken the verse out of context and missed the author's intent. This didn't bother Wayne at all. God spoke to him on the dock, led him to the Gospel of John, and guided him to a specific verse for a specific message. He had asked God for a clear answer and received it. He wasn't going to question God's methods.

Wayne said a short prayer of thanksgiving and climbed out of the car. He softly reentered the tent and snuggled close to Ranae with a revitalized smile. Where else shall I go?

Chapter 32

The Dallas Police officer issued Kurt a $215
speeding ticket. The officer had no idea Kurt had forced a
car off the road in Mesquite. Kurt had the option of
appearing in court on the 23rd of June, attending defensive
driving class, or paying the ticket online. After explaining
these options to Kurt, the officer encouraged Kurt to slow
down and bid the boys a good night.

"What a douche," said John Paul.

"I deserved it," said Kurt. I probably deserve a lot
worse."

"That was nothing. One time my Cousin Akeem
nearly slammed into the back of some lady when we were
warping her. He had to drive into a corn field to avoid her.
Another time, some guy chased us."

"I thought you said no one ever freaked out like that
before?"

"Well," John Paul said, laughing. "I've never seen anyone do that."

"You're an asshole."

"So you're going to pay the ticket?"

"Yeah, I guess. Either that or go to defensive driving."

"No. Don't do that. Go to court and fight it."

"But I was speeding. I have no defense."

"You should go to court anyway. If the officer doesn't show up they'll dismiss your ticket. These cops don't have time to go to court every day. If they showed up every time a ticket went to court they'd never have time to give tickets. If you just show, you got a ninety percent chance of getting it dismissed."

In early June, Kurt received a letter from the court pushing his court date off to July 18th. In the meantime, Kurt worked as many overtime hours as possible to earn money for UTD, but primarily to keep his lovesick mind off Julie. He hadn't heard from her since she left him at the curb. They hadn't gone this long without contact since the eighth grade. He convinced Elio and John Paul to lift weights with him in the evenings, but John Paul quit after the first week.

Kurt also spent more time in the back yard with Monica. She had been begging Kurt to play with her since she had started playing soccer, but he had only spent a few minutes playing with her. After his last date with Julie, however, they played whenever Kurt was home. At first Kurt played all-time goalie and let her beat him, but eventually Kurt refused to play games. Instead, Kurt led her in soccer drills and conditioning exercises. After a few weeks Monica seemed to invent chores and extra credit homework to avoid Kurt's tutelage.

Kurt's monotonous shifts at Maples Industry were interminable. The repetition of the assembly line die-press shifted his mind into neutral. Every thirty seconds he grabbed a flat piece of metal from the right conveyor belt, laid it in the metal die, and pushed both buttons simultaneously. The ten ton press bent the piece of metal at a right angle. He then placed the altered piece of metal on the left conveyor belt which led to six more presses before becoming a transmission part. He repeated the process for twelve hours a day, four days a week. He was a prisoner of his own mind and Julie was his constant cellmate.

On a hot Friday in mid-July, Monica's soccer team competed in a tournament in Plano. Kurt volunteered to take Monica to the game, to relieve Mrs. Hitzges, who had been driving thirty-five minutes to the fields and back all week. The Pink Lightning had won their group and advanced to the final game against the Shortcakes, a team from Plano. Kurt walked the sidelines nervously, anxious to see if their backyard sessions had any affect.

The game was tight early on. Both teams scored a goal within the first ten minutes, then the game settled into a defensive stalemate. With five minutes left in the first half, the referee missed a penalty that should have given the Pink Lightning a penalty kick. Several parents booed and screamed for a foul. Kurt frowned and shook his head.

The game remained tied into the last ten minutes of the game. The Shortcakes carried the ball into the offensive zone. Within an inch of the spot where the call was missed in the first half, a Pink Lightning defender fouled a

Shortcake. The ref raised her arm and called for a penalty kick. The Pink Lightning bleachers erupted in protest, but Kurt's voice rose above them all, "You got to call it the same both ways!" yelled Kurt. "Did you get a new rule book this half?"

The ref seized the ball, walked it to the eighteen, and set it down for a penalty kick.

"If you're only going to let Plano teams win, why did you even invite us?" yelled Kurt.

After placing the ball on the "X," the ref turned her head to stare at Kurt. The Shortcake player took the penalty kick and poked the ball into the lower left corner of the net, putting the Shortcakes ahead by a goal.

Kurt knew he had gotten under the ref's skin and wanted to dig a little more. "Are you on the Plano City Council or do they pay you to fix games? That's bullshit!"

The ref sternly looked at the coach and pointed at Kurt. "Coach," she yelled, "you need to remove that parent from the park."

Kurt's heart jumped. Me? he thought. We were all yelling. I'm not even a parent. Why is she kicking me out?

The coach looked at Kurt. "Please leave. Now. She won't resume the game till you've gone."

As Kurt turned to go he caught a glimpse of Monica, her head bowed in embarrassment. Kurt walked to the parking lot in a daze. What just happened? he wondered. How have I become the kind of person who gets kicked out of a U8 soccer game? The kind of person who publicly humiliates his little sister? I'm not *that* guy. Am I? Kurt searched for answers.

His obsession with Julie was the bitter thread running through his life over the past year. His slide began when he decided to be the prize. I can't be the person she wants, he thought. I have enough trouble being a nice guy. Why did I think I could be a tough guy? Before Julie left for college, we had an unbreakable bond. A lifetime friendship. I've managed to offend everyone close to me. John Paul is the only one who likes me better as an asshole. Kurt retrieved his phone from his pocket and texted Julie:

I have been such a jerk lately. I am sorry. I need to see you. Please. I know I've made you hate me every time I've seen you lately but give me one more chance. Please.

When the game ended, Kurt rushed back to the soccer field. He found Monica and grabbed her soccer bag, slinging it over his shoulder. "How did it turn out?" asked Kurt. "Did you girls come back?"

Monica walked swiftly past him, "No," she said.

"I'm sorry about what happened. I was acting stupid. It won't happen again."

Monica looked up at Kurt and smiled graciously. "It's okay. The coach said you were right. They should have given us a penalty kick."

"How about some ice cream?"

"Sure."

Kurt's phone beeped. It was Julie:

I could never hate you.

Kevin Cobb

> *I'm in Austin for the weekend but I'll be back*
> *Monday. Come over around 8?*

On the drive home Kurt was struck with the memory of running a car off the road and fleeing the scene. Instead of being remorseful, he had hatched a scheme to cheat his way out of a speeding ticket on a technicality. What have I become? When they arrived home he went to his room and found the speeding ticket. In dark italicized print it read:

> *Online payments must be received within 10*
> *days of court date.*

It was already July 14th, just four days before his court date. He had also missed the cutoff for defensive driving class. Only two options remained, attending the court date or paying the fine in person.

Kurt drove to Julie's house on Monday evening. She met Kurt at the front door, and they sat together on her front porch. The sun was in their eyes. It was less than a half hour from setting and the wind had quit. Kurt was sweating and uncomfortable. After uneasy small talk, Julie pushed the conversation along. "So what's up?"

"Well," said Kurt, "I mostly need to apologize to you. I haven't been myself for the past several months, and I've treated you poorly. You've been nothing but great to me, and I've nearly destroyed our friendship."

A neighbor started his lawn mower two doors down, causing both Kurt and Julie to glance to the left. Julie turned back and looked intently into Kurt's eyes with no signs of neither malice nor good will.

"I've treated you just awfully the past several months," Kurt continued. "I've tried to change who I am to be what I think you want me to be. I've always been the nice guy. The dependable guy everyone wants as a friend, but not as a boyfriend. I thought I was a pushover, so I tried to act gritty and indifferent. I had crazy hopes of making you jealous." Kurt looked down at the chipped, grey lacquer on the seasoned oak porch. "But that was childish," he continued. "That was stupid. I've been trying to be something I'm not, and it turns out I don't make a likable tough guy. People say I'm a nice guy. I don't know if that's true anymore. So I'm just a guy. I wish I was someone you preferred as something more than a friend, but regardless, this is all I am."

Kurt wiped the beaded sweat off his forearm and subtly rubbed it onto his shorts. "You and I get along so well," he said. "At least we used to. We clicked like no one else I've ever known. Until recently, conversation with you has always been effortless. I always hear married people say that they married their best friend."

Julie's eyes widened in astonishment.

"Whoa!" Kurt laughed. "Don't worry. Sorry. No. I'm not here to propose. I promise. But still, I couldn't live with myself if I didn't ask one more time. I wish you'd give me a try, just give *us* a chance. We can take it as slowly as you like. When you were in Florida, I was a mess. I missed you so much when you were gone."

Kurt looked down again, then back into Julie's eyes. "But I can't chase you anymore," he said. "I hope and wish you feel the same, but if you don't want this, I'll just have to find a way to deal with it. You mean everything to me, but this chase is miserable. I think the world of you, but I don't want anything from you that you don't want to freely give me."

Julie paused for a long time and looked out into the neighborhood with profound deliberation. After blinking hard she turned to Kurt. "You can't read me at all, can you?" she said with an ironic smile. "Since the year we met I've been in love with you. Always. I feel safe when I'm with you. You make me smile when I'm having a bad day. Life just seems easy when we're together. Like you said, we talk effortlessly. I don't have that with anyone else."

Kurt's heart raced and a new hope lifted his soul. Julie looked out at the neighborhood again then back at Kurt. "Even so," she said, "I fear what might happen if we ever became a couple. Everything would change. Once we go down that road there's no turning back. These things only go one of two ways. Either we spend our lives together and live happily ever after, or somewhere along the line the fire burns out, our love goes bad, and we never see each other again. Friendship over. You're not *one* of my best friends Kurt, you're my *best* friend. I can't lose that. I can't. I've told you a thousand times, not as an excuse, but because it's the truth. This awkwardness the past year is exactly what I was afraid of. I backed off because I don't want to lose you. But I've hated it. I've missed you too, more than you can know."

Julie gently placed her hand on top of his. "We're only nineteen," she said. "Aren't we too young to take that risk? How many people meet their wife in the eighth grade? Don't we need to get our hearts broken by other people first? By the time we finish college we'll have exes and ugly breakup stories. If we're still single by then, it could be something special. What's the rush?"

Kurt's mood was dampened and images of ex-boyfriends filled his mind. "Yeah," he said. "There's no rush, I've waited six years. What's another three?"

Julie laughed. "I don't think I can wait *that* long. Let's just take things slow and see what happens. If I stay in Dallas, who knows? But I don't even know where I'm going to school next month," said Julie. "Honestly. I really haven't decided. My parents still want me to go to UTD, and I'm leaning that way, but I'm afraid I'm making a decision based on where *you* are. I know too many people who picked a school based on a relationship and later regretted it."

"No. I can't let you do that." said Kurt. "You have to pick a school for *you*."

"Yes. I don't know how I'm going to make a sensible decision, but I have to think this through."

Julie took Kurt's hand and they stood. She put her hands on Kurt's shoulders, and Kurt put his hands on her waist. Julie looked into Kurt's eyes. "If you ever decide to be someone else," said Julie sarcastically, "make sure it's not John Paul. I'd rather you take after Elio. His eyes are much prettier."

Kurt looked down in embarrassed laughter, but he was relieved by her levity. "From now on I'll just be me," he said.

Julie looked into Kurt's eyes with an amused smile, then her expression turned solemn. "I have to make some serious decisions," she said. "You need to give me time to digest all this. I'm registered at two schools right now. I need to pick one and stick to it. There's so much going through my head right now. More than I can make sense of. Give me a chance to sort it all out. Please."

Kurt leaned in and rested his chin on her forehead. "Take as long as you need."

Julie smiled, and they shared a long hug. She kissed him on the cheek and disappeared into the house.

Chapter 33

Three hours after Zoe called, Steve was lying in bed at Our Lady of Angels. A nurse drew his blood, then shaved and scrubbed him from neck to toe. When Andy arrived, an IV was being placed in Steve's right hand. Andy smiled and spoke encouragingly, but Steve still read anxiety in his eyes.

Steve was delighted when a nurse told him she would be removing his dreaded PICC line, but it also served as a sobering reminder that his fate was sealed. There was no turning back. What am I doing? he thought. Am I ready to risk it all? I may live another year or two without surgery, maybe three or four. Is it actually possible to remove a beating heart from a human, put it into another, and restart it? It sounds absurd.

Steve visualized an ambulance zooming across town with his new heart in a Coleman cooler. Or, a speeding ambulance barrels through a busy intersection and is hit by a ten ton bulldozer. A magnitude 9.5 earthquake rocks the hospital, causing the unstable surgeon to make an errant and deadly incision. A drunk surgeon drops the handoff from a nurse and his new heart is on the operating room floor. The surgeon opens the cooler and there is no heart. The surgeon opens the cooler to find a black heart. The surgeon opens the cooler to find a liver. The surgeon opens Steve's chest and realizes that transposition patients can't receive heart transplants.

The nurse returned, but did not remove his PICC line. Instead, she picked up the phone beside his bed. "The surgeon would like to talk to you, Mr. Dunham," she said, handing the phone to Steve. The nurse exited the room as soon as Steve took the receiver.

"Mr. Dunham," said a serious male voice.

"Yes?" said Steve.

"Hello, this is Dr. Mino. I'm the surgeon on call this weekend."

"Uh, yes. Hi."

"Mr. Dunham, I hate to disappoint you, but this is not a viable heart for you. Hopefully we'll get you a healthy heart real soon."

Steve was confounded. Only minutes before he had conjured up legitimate excuses to delay surgery, but the doctor's news brought no relief. Conversely, he received the news as a personal affront. Something intimate and precious had been given to him, only to be snatched away.

"What do you mean?" asked Steve.

"The heart is not viable. After a closer investigation, this heart isn't a good match for you. It's better that we figure that out now rather than when you're on bypass."

Steve remained silent for several moments before he responded. "So I just go home then?"

"Yes, sir. I'm sorry. Three hearts have already come in this week. Stay positive. Hopefully we'll get you one soon."

Andy and Steve didn't say a word on the mystified ride home. The doctor's explanation perplexed Steve. Dark despair plagued his mind, and he thought of a thousand reasons why he would never receive a heart.

He looked down at the awkward and cumbersome PICC line with disdain. Steve's spirit dropped to new lows, and paranoia captivated his mind. He was convinced the doctor had canceled his surgery because of the rare and complex nature of the surgery due to his transposition. He doubted if Dr. Mino or any other surgeon would ever operate on him. An overwhelming need to salvage lost time washed over Steve, but time was running out.

When Ashley returned from her trip, Steve insisted that Cornelius remain with him since he was home most of the time. Steve walked slower and shorter distances, but promptly responded whenever Cornelius scratched at the door.

Steve walked Cornelius toward the cemetery, deep in thought about the healthy heart he had lost. He was convinced the heart was withheld from him and given to a patient with a less complicated medical history. Dr. Mino knew the condition of my heart before I was called in, he thought. Why did he change his mind two hours later? Maybe Dr. Mino didn't look at my file until after I was called. He took one look at my chart and backed out. He doesn't want to be responsible for killing me. I don't blame him. I'm a hot potato. What if months and years pass and I'm still on the list? Have I been blackballed? I'll be one of the guys with black and blue legs, too weak to walk. I'm already too weak to teach; how will I support myself?

Weeks passed without another call from the clinic, and Steve resigned himself to his deeply held suspicion that he would never receive a heart or else he would die in surgery. I'll never see my grandchildren, he thought. What will Becca say about me to her future children? Will Andy tell them of these past couple of months or is my legacy of selfishness all that will remain? Good men with devoted families are forgotten within a generation or two. How long before the traces of my selfish existence vanish? Ten years? Five? Will they remember the anniversary of my death?

Steve pulled out his yellow legal pad and penned another letter. He sealed it in an envelope and carried it to the mailbox. He returned to the house sweating and breathing hard. When he reached the recliner, he flopped with a moan. He picked up his phone to search for a number. After catching his breath, he tapped the call button.

"What do you want?" said a female voice.

"Veronica?"

"What do you want, Steve?" asked Veronica.

"I know you don't want to hear from me. I won't keep you long." Steve waited for a response, but only heard silence. "Uh, I'm not sure what to say," he continued. "You know all my tricks and my flaws. I've lied to you and deceived you and hurt you in so many ways over and over again. You can never trust my promises and my candor, and I don't blame you." Steve paused again, greeted by more uncomfortable silence. "I'm babbling. Sorry. Um, I just, I just want to apologize for destroying our marriage, for hurting you in ways I don't even know. I deprived our kids of a father. You deserved better, and I'm glad you found a good husband. Andy has told me how good Jake is to you. I'm sincerely happy for you. I'm just trying to say I'm sorry."

"You think you can clean up a lifetime of neglect with a phone call?" said Veronica. "You're not interested in bringing me peace. I found my peace a long time ago, without *your* help. Frankly I'm revolted that you're dragging it all up again. This phone call is all about *you*, Steve. You're not concerned with my feelings. As always, it's about *you*. Well, I'm not letting you off that easy. I'm not letting you off period. When you die, I won't shed a single tear." She abruptly hung up.

Steve shriveled into the recliner and laid his phone on the floor. Of course, she's right, he thought. She's right. She couldn't possibly benefit from that call. Selfish. I did it for *my* peace, not hers. He thought about the letter he'd just sent to Becca. He was sincere, but it was still laced with a selfish agenda.

Each weekend, an unspoken optimism was in the air at Steve's house. Organ donations spike on weekends. Recreation vehicles such as boats, ATV's, and motorcycles are used much more often on the weekends. Gunshot victim are more common on weekends. But the greatest contributions come as a result of drunk drivers and reckless teenagers.

A transplanted heart must come from a beating heart donor, thus, heart donors are brain dead but breathing when their organs are harvested. Steve had missed the fertile prom season, and the homecoming season was months away. He couldn't imagine waiting till then. Each Friday Steve's hope and optimism blossomed, but his new-found consciousness reprimanded his ego for indirectly wishing the death of a stranger.

Steve was desperate to apologize to Andy for his years of negligence, but his inexperience at humbling himself and the recent conversation with Veronica prevented him from approaching Andy. Am I apologizing for his benefit or mine? he wondered. The situation with Andy was different than with Veronica, wasn't it? Despite the harm he had inflicted upon Andy in decades past, they had nurtured a meaningful relationship. Andy had even moved into his home.

The call to Veronica was disastrous, but it didn't excuse him from apologizing to Andy. He had already initiated a conversation with Steve about the unsettled past. Andy deserved reconciliation. Each passing day on the heart list was a lost opportunity. His silence became more agonizing than a confession.

The Fourth of July weekend failed to yield a heart, and Steve reached thirty days on the list. Each passing day cemented Steve's belief that he would never receive a new heart. His appetite left him, and he struggled to find energy; nevertheless, he walked Cornelius every day. Andy joined Steve whenever possible and limited their journeys to a trip around the block.

One Saturday morning, Steve exited his bedroom to the welcoming aroma of coffee, but Andy was nowhere around. Steve assumed he had left early. Maybe he went to see Ashley at the apartment. When he walked to the coffee pot, however, he was greeted by a blue sticky note on the coffee maker:

Grab a cup and meet me outside

Intrigued, Steve walked out onto the driveway. Andy stood by Steve's truck, which was attached to Steve's fishing boat.

"Come on, old man," Andy said with a wide smile. "You must have twenty packs of those damn Blue fleck Powerworms. Why don't you show me how to use them?"

At the boat launch, Andy backed the boat into the lake, unhooked it, and maneuvered it to the dock while Steve sat passively in the passenger seat. Andy parked the truck and accompanied Steve to the dock. Andy crouched on the dock to untie the boat. He sat on the dock and pinned the boat to the dock with his feet, keeping it from drifting. Steve cautiously sat beside him.

"Put your hand on my shoulder," said Andy. "Let me hold your pump."

"No," said Steve. "I got it." He was still catching his breath from sitting down. After a few deep breaths he leaned heavily upon Andy's shoulder and placed his feet on the bottom of the boat. Andy's feet kept the boat fast against the dock as the two men worked together to get

Steve into the boat. He held Steve steady until he sat safely in the bow.

The lake was glass. Andy navigated the small boat out of the marina and into the open lake.

"Where to?" asked Andy.

"When did you learn to drive a boat?" said Steve. "I didn't know you'd ever been on the water except with me. Fishing camp?"

Andy laughed. "I learned yesterday. I took it out with Phil from work. He fishes all the time. He showed me how to hook up the boat and how to operate it."

"Do you want me to drive?"

"It's a boat, it's not rocket science."

"Okay then," said Steve, surveying the lake. "We don't need to go far. Just take us over there to the riprap along the bridge."

"What's riprap?"

"You see all those large stones piled up along the bridge?"

"Yeah."

"That's riprap."

Steve taught Andy how to work a plastic worm along the bank, and he tied a spinnerbait onto his own line. The sun rose higher and poured on the heat. Though he was rapidly losing energy, Steve was ensconced in bliss.

The two fished along the bridge for half an hour without a bite. Steve recognized the unspoken responsibility of keeping a novice fisherman entertained. "Sorry we're not getting any bites," said Steve. "I haven't been here in so long I'm not sure where the black bass are hiding these days. Maybe we should try black worms or maybe a lipless crankbait. Pass me the tackle box and I'll change out your bait."

Andy laughed. "Take it easy. It's nice just being out here with you. If I catch a fish, I want it to be on one of your Powerworms."

Steve cast his spinnerbait under a small tree hanging over the water. The heavy bait landed directly in the shadow, and his rod immediately twitched violently. He reeled in some slack and yanked the rod. Steve knew it was a small fish. He finessed the largemouth alongside the hull and hoisted the emerald green fish into the boat. Steve scrambled to place his hand in the fish's mouth, lipping it. He lifted the fish with his own mouth agape, struggling to catch his breath.

"Hell yeah!" Andy said, searching the bottom of the boat for his phone.

"I was hoping *you'd* catch the first one," said Steve.

"Are you kidding?" Andy said. "We're out here for you." Andy adjusted his phone to take a picture. "Hold it up."

Steve laughed. "No," he said. "It's a keeper, but this little guy wouldn't go two pounds."

"Come on, hold it up. When's the last time you caught a fish with your son?"

Conscious of his pump, Steve tucked his tubing behind his back and raised the fish.

"Hold your pump up too."

"No, that's embarrassing."

"Come on now. Like you said, that's not exactly a fish worth telling stories about. You've caught dozens bigger. But how many people have ever caught a bass while connected to a milrinone pump? Come on, hold it up."

Steve proudly held up the eyesore of a pump, and Andy took a picture of his father, a bass in one hand, a pump in the other. Steve gently placed the fish into the warm water by the lip and rocked the bass gently back and forth, moving oxygen through his gills. The lively fish darted away from the boat in a flash.

Steve sat heavily to catch his breath. He turned to his son. "I'm sorry, Andy. I'm so very sorry. After everything I've put you through, I don't deserve a fishing trip. I failed you. I failed you and I failed Becca. I've lived my life for me and me alone. Your mother was terrific. I never should have left her. I never should have left any of you. My responsibility was to my family, but I remained a child and failed you all. I've been so selfish. But you never quit. If you hadn't reached out to me over and over again, if you hadn't—" Steve paused to catch his breath, but before he found his voice again, Andy put his arm around him.

"It's okay, Dad," said Andy. "You've said plenty, thank you. I have you *now*, Dad. All these years I've never been looking for apologies or any kind of reparations. I just wanted *you*. That's all that matters to me. I'm so glad you're in my life."

Steve crumpled in exhaustion. He focused on his breathing and tried to relax. Andy walked to the front of the boat and retracted the trolling motor. He started the engine, and the two headed merrily home.

Kevin Cobb

Chapter 34

When Steve opened the golden door, the luminous glow forced him to squint. The iridescent white dome illuminating the immaculate lobby rivaled the U.S. Capitol rotunda in both size and splendor. Steve proceeded to the white marble reception desk ten feet into the lobby.

An angel greeted him warmly and pointed him toward a door on the opposite side of the lobby. "Your door is on the left," said the angel.

Steve nodded and walked briskly toward the door on the left side of the far wall. He saw a second portal on the right side of the same wall. His shiny black Florsheims clicked along the golden marble floor, echoing throughout the cavernous dome. He glanced back at the desk, but both the desk and the angel had disappeared. The entrance had vanished as well. He was alone.

The trek was deceptively long. Steve seemed to have travelled twice the distance to the entryway, yet it was as far away as when he entered the mammoth structure, an optical illusion similar to boating across a large lake. He craved rest, but the lobby had no benches, couches, nor recliners. He trudged on, eventually arriving at the passage to the left. Above the huge bronze door was a single word:

Admission

Steve pushed open the ponderous and stubborn door, revealing a stairwell crowded with elderly climbers, sluggishly ascending the steps. The ascending passageway echoed with wheezing, panting, and moaning. It smelled of mildew and damp limestone. The extensive single flight of stairs rose to the equivalent of four floors off the ground. Several of the elderly voyagers carried burdensome oxygen tanks. No one breathed quietly; some sat on the stairs to catch their breath while others passed indifferently.

Steve commenced scaling the gloomy staircase with great trepidation. The first step nearly tripped him. Each concrete step stood nearly four inches taller than standard steps and flared outward so that each step tapered into a ledge. After but a few steps, Steve was winded.

The stairway appeared crowded, but each climber was taking an isolated journey of his or her own. Four steps ahead, a fragile woman in her late seventies struggled along. She might as well have been a half mile away. He wouldn't arrive at the step she stood on for several minutes. Two men and another woman had already begun their own ascent behind him. There was no turning back. He knew he was waiting in line for something, but he didn't know what.

Every six to eight steps, Steve sat down and placed his hands behind his neck to breathe easier. Some climbers sat to rest, but lacked the strength to stand again. Instead, they scooted themselves from step to step from a sitting position.

Steve and the lady ahead looked at each other with mutual sympathy as they gasped for air, mouths wide open, too winded to verbally communicate. He noticed the woman had medical tubing running into a fanny pack around her waist. She had a milrinone pump. Steve perused the stairwell and observed that everyone was attached to a pump. He suddenly became aware of his own milrinone pump, tucked into the pocket of his cargo shorts. Steve and his fellow heart patients were mysteriously compelled to press on by an unseen force.

Steve passed five people worse off than himself. He wanted to stop and help, but feared a delay would hinder him from completing his own climb. After several rest breaks, Steve eyed the stairwell landing five steps ahead. With relief in sight, he gathered the energy to reach the top.

An ancient oval door, trimmed in diamonds, served as the stairwell exit. Steve passed through the opulent door and doubled over with his hands on his hips to catch his breath once again. He was delighted to see that the line of patients in front of him stood on level ground. He followed the line into a room that appeared to be the antithesis of the lobby. It was domed as well, but the room was more like a dingy stone cavern, the lighting was poor, the air dank. In the middle of this commodious room was a grey rustic shed. The line of patients stretched fifty feet to a single door on the left side of the tiny shed. The door opened occasionally and patients entered the shed one by one.

An elevator door opened to the left of the stairwell, and a man in blue medical scrubs emerged from the elevator pushing a patient on a gurney. The pale woman had no blanket, exposing her swollen, black and purple legs. The man hastily forced the patient to the front of the line and into the shed.

Is this where I get a new heart? Steve wondered. He was both frightened and anxious with the prospect of an immediate transplant. Two dozen patients stood between the shed and himself. For the first time he noticed a second line of patients coming from the right and entering the shed on the opposite side. Both lines dwindled, and more patients arrived on gurneys, preempting the line.

As Steve moved closer to the tiny shed, he noticed the patients in the right line were significantly younger and didn't appear to be patients at all. They all looked young, beautiful, and athletic. They also appeared to be confused and frustrated. Some wore sports attire, business suits, and medical uniforms. Others were dressed for farm work, construction, and all manner of labor. Several of the youth talked and texted on their phones while others looked at their watches. Some stared inquisitively at the shed.

Kevin Cobb

A cold wave ran down Steve's spine when he realized the purpose of the second line. He dropped his head in shame, embarrassed to be seen by the donors. The right line abounded with young healthy adults in the prime of their lives, poised to conquer the world.

The left line comprised of broken down senior citizens whose hopes and dreams had been played out long ago. Steve was three decades younger than most everyone else in the left line, yet he was still much older than those standing to the right. Some looked too young to be out of high school. He wondered if any of his former students waited in line. Steve was ashamed and viewed himself unworthy to take the place of a vigorous and ambitious youth.

Although he was ashamed, Steve held his life too dearly to relinquish his chance at a new heart, so he stayed in line, keeping his eyes on the feet of the lady in front of him. Still, he was embarrassed to be associated with this selfish and unworthy group. We had our chance to live, he thought. We have no right to steal theirs.

He couldn't face the donors as a group, but he also dreaded the thought of seeing the individual who would involuntarily forgo a life for Steve. How could he justify his privilege to trade hearts? He had lived a full life, at least twenty years more than most of them. He had loved and lost and loved again, many times. He had traveled the world, he had offspring to be remembered by. He had grabbed his opportunities, capitalizing on some, busting on many others, but what about these kids? It was their turn to live.

Three patients stood between Steve and the macabre shed. The elevator opened, and another gurney was rushed to the front of the line. Moments later Steve looked directly at the shed. He was next. He looked up without disgrace because he stood too close to the shed to see the donors on the other side.

Wait a minute, he thought. What am I doing? I had a chance to thank my donor in person, to express my gratitude. Instead, I cowered in shame.

Steve stepped out of line and walked toward the donor side of the shed. Instantly, an angel appeared directly in front of him.

"You're next in line, sir," said the angel. "Please step back in line."

"Yes, okay," said Steve. "First let me thank my donor. It'll just take a second."

"Please step back in line."

"I must thank my donor first." Steve attempted to sidestep the angel, but the angel mirrored his lateral movement, still standing directly in front of him. Steve attempted to push the angel aside, but the divine creature was solid as the trunk of a sturdy oak. Steve turned around and ran back toward the stairwell. "Never mind!" he yelled. "I don't want a heart anymore! Keep it! Let them all keep it!"

Before Steve made it four steps the angel appeared directly in his path yet again. As Steve came to a halt, the shed door opened. Gale force winds blew him toward the door. It took but a moment to realize the wind wasn't blowing, but sucking. A great force pulled him toward the door. He grabbed the feet of the angel to prevent being swallowed by the shed.

Out of the corner of his eye, Steve saw the donors. Their door was also open, and both lines were being pulled into the shed. The ambition once present in the youthful eyes was replaced by terror. They were abruptly confronted with certain and immediate death. Some screamed obscenities and cursed God. Others cried uncontrollably, grasping and clutching the floor around them, but there was nothing to cling to, nothing to stop them from fulfilling their destiny.

The elderly patients also screamed and protested, afraid of the unknown. After several moments of chaos, both lines disappeared into the mysterious shed. Only Steve remained, defiantly clinging to the angel's legs. The angel reached down and gently gripped Steve's hands, lifting him to eye level. Steve's body flailed in the wind like a flag.

Kevin Cobb

Steve looked directly into the soft eyes of the white-haired angel. "I don't deserve a heart," Steve screamed over the deafening gale.

"No one deserves a heart," said the angel with a compassionate smile.

The angel released Steve's hands, and he disappeared into the shed with the rest of the patients and donors.

Chapter 35

Wayne woke up at Purtis Creek enthusiastic and energized. He still had unanswered questions, but a peace he hadn't experienced since his earliest days at Vandyke comforted his soul. God had brought him through trials of faith to galvanize him for the ministry. He was ready to speak boldly of the things of God with a clear conscience. When the Davidsons returned to Dallas, however, Wayne's mind slid back into the same cynical outlook he thought he had left for dead on the L shaped dock.

Becca recognized Steve's messy handwriting when she opened the mailbox. She sighed loudly and ascended the tope carpeted staircase to her apartment. She knew she would open *this* letter. Andy had texted her the day before, begging her to open the next letter from their father as a favor to him. She reluctantly promised Andy she would.

Becca sat on the sofa staring at the envelope, shaking her head in disgust. Finally she ripped the envelope open:

Rebecca

I owe you the most sincere apology. I am a selfish man and have spent my life living for my own frivolous desires. I was blessed with a great wife, beautiful children, and a promising life. I threw it all away because I'm a selfish jerk. You and your brother deserved so much better. I am sorry I robbed you of a loving father. I want to change, and I am trying to change. God only knows if I have enough time. I have forfeited every right to your love and affection, and it is my burden to live with. I ask nothing of you. May my feeble attempt to make amends provide you with a measure of comfort.

I love you,

Steve

"Bastard!" Becca said, standing and pacing. She read the letter again, chewing on her cuticles. She stopped at her desk and read the letter one more time then wadded the letter and dropped it into the waste basket.

When Kurt returned from Julie's house, a torrent of thoughts and emotions crowded his mind. Throughout the night, he searched unsuccessfully for a comfortable position. The positivity he carried from Julie's porch had turned sour in his stomach.

Why did I have to make a big speech like that? Kurt thought. I gave her an ultimatum. I should have kept cool and waited for the tension to pass.

But another voice reminded Kurt she had confessed she was in love with him. They were the words I've wanted to hear for years, he thought, but she was still talking about returning to Florida. I can't face three more years of phone tag and I'm sure as hell not going to lay back and patiently wait for her to collect ex-boyfriends. If she returns to Florida it's over, but if she stays, the sky's the limit.

The warring introspection kept his mind running at full speed throughout the night. Just before sunrise, he considered getting up, but his head pounded with fatigue. Instead, he rolled over and fell asleep.

Chapter 36

July 18, 2018

12:07 p.m.

Wayne sat in his office staring blankly at his computer. The only show in town? he thought. How do I know that? I've been studying Christianity for years, and I still haven't fully wrapped my arms around the simplest Christian doctrines. How can I dismiss other religions and philosophies out of hand? I've studied Islam and Judaism as a solider surveys enemy lines. I could teach a class on their history and core doctrines, but that's about it. What do I really know? And what about more unfamiliar religions? I don't even understand the essence of Buddhism or any other Eastern philosophy. My thinking is just too black and white.

Wayne stood anxiously and paced the cozy office. He opened the closet mindlessly and pulled a driver from his golf bag. He stood in the most spacious part of the office, bent his knees, and addressed an imaginary ball, holding the club firm with his uninjured right hand.

Where else shall we go? he thought. Only You have the words of everlasting life. Where else shall I go? I can't speak this with conviction unless I've objectively studied all the best alternatives, or at least *some* alternatives. If I can understand these other philosophies and still hold to Christianity, then I'll have perfect peace. I'll know that only *You* have the words of everlasting life.

As he began a slow back swing, he watched the head of the club, making sure he didn't hit the ceiling fan. Wayne straightened his stance abruptly and leaned the club against the wall. He looked at the middle book shelf, perusing various titles. Stooping, he found the Quran on the bottom shelf amidst the Eightfold Path, the Book of Mormon, and the Mishna. He had bought these books to defend Christ before his enemies from a fully educated position, but he scanned the shelf with no intentions of defending or destroying anything. He just wanted to understand.

He grabbed the Quran and sat at his desk. Flipping through the table of contents, he was surprised that it carried no familiarity. It was nothing like the Bible. He could generally explain the five pillars of Islam, but had never looked at the Quran itself. He opened to the first page:

Surah I

The Opening

1.   In the Name of Allah, the Beneficent, the Merciful.

2.   All praise is due to Allah, the Lord of the Worlds.

3.   The Beneficent, the Merciful

4.   Master of the Day of Judgment

5.   Thee do we serve and Thee do we beseech for help.

6.   Keep us on the right path.

7.   The path of those upon whom Thou hast bestowed favors. Not (the path) of those upon whom Thy wrath is brought down, nor of those who go astray.

Kevin Cobb

Wayne read the passage several times convinced the text couldn't be any more confusing if it had been written in the original Arabic. His eyes drew down to the title of next passage:

Selah II, The Cow.

He closed the book and tossed it onto the desk. Where do I begin? he thought. I have no context. It's like someone reading the Bible from the beginning, hoping to understand Christianity from the Book of Genesis. He had been naive to think he could truly understand *all* religions. When it comes down to it, he thought, I don't even fully understand Protestant Christianity. I only understand one small strain of it. Actually, just one small part of Evangelical Christianity. I've not even fully explored the many manifestations of my own faith.

12:51 p.m.

Steve walked into the garage searching for Cornelius's leash. The cluttered garage held the Texas heat, and sweat beaded on Steve's forehead. His eye drifted to the blue bike leaning against the wall. He ran his hand along the rear tire to feel the coarse and tacky tread. Shortly after he had been diagnosed with heart failure, he replaced nearly bald tires with a new set. Back then, optimism flowed from him like a faucet. With a new lease on life and a renewed commitment to an active lifestyle, he had intended to wear out another set or two before his heart needed replaced, but just three months after he bought the tires, he was too weak to ride.

What a waste, he thought. He moved his thumb back and forth over the tread. He hadn't even worn down the tiny black tabs surrounding the periphery of the tires. He wished he had the strength to wear out another set or at least scuff it up a bit, at least enough to wear off the little black tabs.

Steve opened the garage and led the bike down the driveway and into Bollywood Avenue. He looked down the street. The paved road dropped away from the house at a subtle angle for about sixty yards before bottoming out and rising slightly toward Sixth Street at about the same angle. The descent in elevation was less than five feet total but it dropped enough to let him coast to the nadir.

With one foot on a pedal and the other on the ground, he sat on the bike. Before he pushed off, he noticed the clumsy tubing running to his arm. He opened the tiny duffle bag, took out the pump, and pulled it back through the arm of his t-shirt. He shoved the pump snuggly into the left cargo pocket of his shorts, tucking the remaining tubing behind the pump.

Steve pushed off and cranked the pedals several revolutions before coasting. The delight of unfettered movement intoxicated him. The wind blew his hair gently, tickling his ears, and he savored the liberating sensation of moving through open space. He floated down the hill like a cottonwood spore, temporarily cheating the afternoon heat. As he neared the low point in street, he didn't want the entertaining ride to end.

Bursting with adrenaline, he pedaled through the shallow dip and up toward the stop sign at the end of the street. Ten yards into the minor ascent, however, his thighs filled with lactic acid and he couldn't catch his breath. He suffered through five more yards and came to an unceremonious halt, placing both feet on the ground.

Catching his breath, he stepped off the bike and sat sweating on the curb. Looking back at the light green house, he knew he'd never make it back home on his own. He texted Andy to pick him up.

As he waited for Andy, the faint recollection of an unnerving dream brushed his consciousness. He recalled long lines of unhappy people, desperate screaming, and a blustering wind. The phantasm became a vivid painting in his mind and the haunted faces of terror turned his stomach. A dark chill grazed Steve's shoulders, provoking a fleeting shiver in the relentless July heat.

1:15 p.m.

Wayne sat in his office finishing a reaction paper for his final summer class. He temporarily pushed aside his spiritual struggle in order to finish his homework. His ring tone chimed, and he looked at his phone. The area code was unfamiliar so he let the call go to voicemail. A church in Illinois was calling about his pastoral résumé. He returned the call right away.

369

"Hello?" said a voice.

"Hello, this is Wayne Davidson. I think you just called me."

"Yes, Wayne. Thanks for getting back with me. This is Clay Davis, a board member at Image Community Church in Woodridge, Illinois. I'm heading up the pastoral search committee. We'd like to know if you're interested in visiting our church for an interview."

"Yes, sir."

Wayne got off the phone in a daze. The church wanted to fly him to Chicago for an interview right away. He promised Clay he would talk with Ranae and call him back within the hour.

1:28 p.m.

When Ranae reached the elevator, a crowd filled the lobby. One of the three elevators was out of service. The large Roman numeral clock above the center elevator reminded her that her lunch break ended in two minutes. She opened the door to the stairwell and began her sprint to the thirteenth floor. As she reached the fourth floor landing her phone rang.

"Hey, babe," said Ranae, slowing to a steady climb. "What's up?"

"I just got a call from a church in Chicago," said Wayne. "They want to interview me for an associate pastor position."

"Chicago? That's great! That's so exciting."

"Actually, it's a suburb. They want us to fly out today at 4:50. Their senior pastor left suddenly. They want to start interviewing right away. We would meet with church members and the church board on Saturday, and I would preach on Sunday morning."

"We? They want *me* to come?"

"Yeah, they're serious. But I didn't answer yet. I know you work till 7:00."

"Don't worry about that, I can work it out. I'll leave right away."

Wayne didn't respond for several seconds. Finally he replied, "I just don't know if I'm ready for this. I haven't even finished my thesis yet."

"You're ready, babe. God has prepared you for this. This is what you were born to do. He's opened a door; let's walk through and see what happens. It's just an interview. Plenty of time to pray about it."

"Yeah, I just don't know if I'm ready."

"You just have cold feet," Ranae said with a laugh. "You'll never feel ready. I didn't think I was ready to work on this floor until I'd been here a couple months. It'll come to you. We have to at least go and visit. I'll get out of here as quick as I can. See you soon."

1:57 p.m.

Brilliant sun invaded Kurt's bedroom window and woke him up. After a few seconds of consciousness, he remembered the previous evening on Julie's porch. She said she loves me, he thought. She might be moving back to Dallas.

He wanted to check his phone, but he didn't dare look. The fear of disappointment outweighed any ecstasy he could imagine from a positive response, and he knew, if she returned to Florida, he was done. She's probably been up for five hours by now, he thought. Maybe she's already made a decision. He reached to the nightstand and looked at his phone. No messages.

Kurt set his phone on the nightstand and ambled downstairs to the kitchen. He opened the refrigerator and perused its contents. He grabbed a bowl from the cabinet and a box of Lucky Charms from the pantry, then back to the refrigerator for milk.

After finishing two bowls, he grabbed a Dr. Pepper and returned to his room. He switched on the PlayStation 4 and sat on his bed. After half an hour of Call of Duty, he looked at his phone. Still nothing. He laid his phone down, but immediately retrieved it to take a second look at the date:

7/18

"Shit!" he screamed. He had missed his 8:00 a.m. court appointment. "Shit, shit, shit!" He snatched the speeding ticket off his desk and ran to the Jeep.

2:13 p.m.

Ranae arrived at the apartment and helped Wayne finish packing. They hauled a large suitcase to the parking lot and loaded it into Wayne's Honda.

Wayne shut the trunk and opened the driver's side door. "We have time to stop at Bailiff. I need to pick up my check. I meant to go get it weeks ago. We may need it this weekend."

"Where do you think *you're* going?" asked Ranae as she walked back to the apartment.

"What?" Wayne asked sarcastically.

"*I'm* driving. I'll be right back. I forgot my purse."

When Ranae returned, Wayne was in the driver's seat, the engine running.

"Get out," said Ranae.

"What?"

"I'm driving, get out. You're not driving."

"I've been driving around town all week. I'm fine."

"No. Your arm's still in a cast. If we're going downtown, I'm driving. Your downtown driving is scary when you have two *good* arms. I'm driving."

"Relax. I'm fine. I drove down to school last week, plus it's the middle of the day. Traffic will be light, I'll be fine."

"Wayne, please. Get out."

"Hop in, it's getting late. We need to go."

Ranae shook her head and climbed into the passenger seat. Although northbound Central expressway was already congested, southbound still flowed freely into the city.

"So what kind of church is it?" Ranae asked.

"It's a Bible church. Independent. Governed by a board of elders."

"What's it called? I'll google it. I want to look for apartments and hospitals tomorrow morning."

"Image Community Church in Woodridge, Illinois."

Ranae began researching on her phone, leaving Wayne alone with his thoughts. What am I doing? Wayne thought. A few days ago I was nearly an atheist; now I'm interviewing to be an assistant pastor? Am I any more confident in my faith than a week ago?

Voltaire and Joseph Butler competed for Wayne's spirit. Heaven? Hell? Nothing? Something else I haven't even imagined? I'm overthinking things. I've learned too much for my own good. Well, I've studied too much for my own good. I'm not sure I've learned anything.

"A two bedroom for $1,750 a month," said Ranae. "Expensive; does that sound about right?"

"Hm."

Ranae looked at Wayne. He was pale and perspiring. He looked agitated. "Babe, relax," she said. "You're a mess. You'll do fine. You've got nothing to worry about. If this doesn't work out something else will come along. Don't put so much pressure on yourself. And slow down, you're speeding."

"Yeah," said Wayne. "We shouldn't have come downtown. We're going to be cutting it close at the airport."

"Do you have a sermon prepared? Do you know what you're going to preach on?"

"From Colossians 3. The one I preached at church last month."

"Oh, good. Yes. That should go well for this." Ranae began scrolling once again. "I wonder how far Woodridge is from Michigan Avenue."

Wayne looked at his resourceful and enthusiastic wife. She's so smart, he thought. So beautiful. And she's in love with *me*. I have so much to enjoy and appreciate, and I spend all my time worrying life away. Too focused on myself. I need to jump into ministry and immerse myself in the needs of other people. When I'm fighting for the needs of a congregation I won't have time for these selfish doubts.

The Live Oak exit was backed up. It took the Davidson's ten minutes to get off the highway. "We're really pushing it now." said Wayne. "We're going to have to valet park at the airport." As soon as Wayne turned onto South Pearl Street he punched the accelerator and buzzed toward Cadiz Street.

"Slow down, Wayne," said Ranae. "Let's skip Bailiff and get back on the freeway."

"No. We're here now. I'll be in and out in two minutes."

"Just slow down!"

2:48 p.m.

Kurt wasn't sure what he'd say or do when he reached the county courthouse, he just knew he had to talk to someone before it closed for the day. Will I be arrested? he wondered. Will I spend the night in jail?

He got off the interstate at the Main Street exit and headed west. As he reached the first stop light, his phone beeped. He looked down and saw that it was a message from Julie. She had made a decision, he hoped, but he didn't have the courage to look at his phone. The light turned green, and he continued to drive. What if she stays in Dallas? What if she transfers to UTD right when I'm starting? The thought was too impossibly blissful to relish. What if she goes back to Florida? But maybe she's texting to say she's staying. Maybe she wants to see me tonight. It was just last night; she probably hasn't even decided yet.

He spotted the large courthouse, but realized he had already overshot the parking lot. His mind was preoccupied with the pivotal text he desperately needed to read. He circled the large edifice and headed west on Commerce Street. Unable to wait any longer, Kurt grabbed the phone and opened the all-important text. His eyes grew large and his heart lurched. He looked back up at the road and the approaching green light. Did I read it correctly? he asked himself.

He looked down to read it again but slower. When he looked up the light had turned red. To his left a speeding gold Honda with two green bumper stickers closed on the driver side door like a heat seeking missile. Kurt mashed his brakes and raised his left hand to block the impending collision. A blinding jolt warmed the left side of his face as he lost consciousness.

Kurt's body was in optimum condition for organ donation. The violent collision damaged some internal organs, nevertheless, seven fortunate recipients received skin grafts. His corneas went to a seventy-three year old man from Fort Worth. His pancreas was successfully transplanted into a teenage girl from Texarkana. A grandfather of eighteen from Waxahachie received a kidney. Kurt's heart was given to a very tall, fifty-one-year-old black man who had lost his son to Leukemia.

When Kurt's Jeep suddenly appeared in the intersection, Wayne attempted to veer to the right but collided hard with the defenseless Jeep. The impact sent Wayne's car careening violently to the left and directly into a solid metal utility pole on the opposite street corner.

Wayne blacked out. When he woke up, thick blood ran down his forehead and into his eyes. He put his hand to his head and felt the moist laceration. To his right, Ranae leaned motionless against the passenger window. Wayne unbuckled his seat belt and crawled onto Ranae's side of the car, cradling her head and leaning back with her into the seat. "Ranae, honey, talk to me. Rabbit. I'm right here. Rabbit. Talk to me, please. Help! Somebody get her an ambulance!"

Bystanders approached the scene quickly, offering assistance and calling for help. When the ambulance arrived, paramedics cleaned and bandaged Wayne's bleeding head. They rushed Ranae to the hospital.

Kevin Cobb

Chapter 37

Wayne felt the sympathetic presence of the numerous church members and Ranae's colleagues who gathered outside Ranae's solemn room, praying and whispering. Wayne sat beside Ranae's bed holding her motionless hand in a surreal state of shock. The doctor had promised him they would do all they could to keep her breathing until her parents arrived from Ohio. He dreaded their appearance, unsure what he'd say. He had failed to perform the most basic duty of any husband.

Ranae's head was heavily bandaged and a cumbersome breathing apparatus covered her mouth, but she still looked like the college girl who had swept Wayne off his feet less than two years earlier. He held her hand with his broken arm and lightly stroked her forearm with the other, occasionally lifting her hand to his cheek. The delicate palm held all of Ranae's warmth, and he was certain she would wake up any minute. He spoke apologies softly into Ranae's ear. He spoke of his love and about his loss. Kiss after kiss he placed on her forehead, on her chin, on her cheek.

Ranae and Steve shared O+ blood. Ranae was over nine inches shorter than Steve, yet her heart fit perfectly. Steve's surgery went smoother than expected. The veins and arteries were of adequate length and required no graphs. Twenty-six hours after surgery, Steve opened his eyes and vaguely recognized Andy sitting next to his bed. He fell back to sleep, but woke an hour later. Again, Andy stood to his right, smiling and holding his hand.

"Welcome back," Andy said. "You look great, Dad."

Steve's sore throat prevented him from speaking, the breathing tube having been removed from his throat just a few minutes earlier. Next to Andy stood a beautiful young lady with long brown hair. With a nervous smile, Becca reluctantly took Steve's hand. "Hi," Becca said with a weak voice. Tears crowded in the corner of Steve's eyes and a grateful smile spanned his face.

Epilogue

Funerals for the elderly are marked with both sadness and joy. It's difficult to bid farewell to an aged loved one, but the sacred ritual affirms nature has run its course and the cycle of life has been successful, the celebration of a life well lived. Conversely, a teenager's funeral is an apocalyptic nightmare, an unnatural tragedy, a total loss.

Elio and John Paul stood in the midst of wailing mourners. Their first taste of an intimate death was still too surreal to feel. The tears weren't ready to come. Kurt's mother, mourning the second death of an immediate family member in four years, held a handkerchief to her eyes with one hand, while cleaving to her sobbing daughter with the other. Mrs. Hitzges was at a total loss, unable to console Monica. Julie stood with dark swollen eyes, but a dry face. In the brief interval between accident and funeral, she had cried a lifetime of tears. There were no tears left to shed.

Kevin Cobb

She was left with an empty heart and a lifetime to dissect each word of the last text she sent Kurt.

       Unable to mourn in peace, Wayne tolerated the many hassles and obligations of being a fresh widower. Before the car was towed from the police impound, Wayne made a final sweep of the vehicle for personal possessions. The sight of the ravaged car unleashed waves of mental agony, and he regretted his decision to inspect the car himself. He pulled the suitcase out of the trunk and left behind the jumper cables and his tattered paperback copy of the Gospel of John. He grabbed a pair of shoes from the back seat and glanced at the passenger side floor mat, freezing him in his tracks. The grief returned anew, reliving the nightmare once again. With a desperately broken heart, he reached down and retrieved a blood-spattered wine cork. He rotated it in his hand until he could read the handwritten inscription:

       Wayne and Ranae, A Lifetime of
Celebrations

Ten months after the transplant, a small seaplane circled a white-capped lake and descended upon a sleepy village. The plane alighted upon the golden surface of a chilly lake in northern Saskatchewan. Steve and Andy were giddy with the prospects of an entire week of fishing the picturesque lake. Becca sat next to Steve with a full heart. She was just happy to spend time with her dad.

The End

Kevin Cobb

Acknowledgments

I must first thank my unknown donor for giving me a chance to live with a healthy heart on October 18, 2014. The heart I was born with stopped beating over three years ago, yet I am still here. Along with your precious heart, it seems you also gave me a love for black coffee, an aversion to steak, and the uncanny ability to learn the guitar. I LIVE GRATEFUL for every breath I take.

I am eternally grateful to my lovely bride, Tricia. When we began dating twenty-eight years ago, I explained to her my heart condition and its potential long-term issues. Tricia didn't flinch. When I proposed, it was with a reminder of my heart issues. Again, she was unfazed. Two decades later my heart failed. Tricia didn't bat an eye and took on the challenge with a demonstration of love and dedication I can never repay. She proved that she was meant to be my guardian angel all along.

Thank you to my beautiful daughters, Liz, Abby, and Sam. You are the very best part of me. You make my

Kevin Cobb

life relevant and you keep me smiling. Thank you for
encouraging me and patiently waiting for me to finish this
book.

Thank you to Rebecca Moore for introducing me to
the beauty of great books and the captivating world of
literature.

Thanks to Shawn Picard, who supported my goofy
idea of writing this book from the very beginning and
cheered me on throughout the entire agonizing process.
Thank you to Matt and Moira Burgy for more than a
decade of pushing me to do things I never thought I could.
Thank you to my friend from birth, Teresa Schiml Forth,
for your valuable feedback.

I would also like to recognize all my former
students. It has been my greatest honor to be a small part of
your lives. A special thanks to Morgan Froehlich, Isabella
Cerritos, Eric Palmerduca, George Nasr and Milan Rabah
for direct contributions to the book.

Thank you to the many competent and caring
people at Baylor University Medical Center in Dallas,
Texas. A special acknowledgement to Juan MacHannaford,

M.D., Sandra Carey, PhD, MPH, CCRN, ANP-BC, Heather Shewmake, MSN, RN, ACNP, and the late Johannes Kuiper, M.D. Thank you to Cincinnati's Children's Hospital for allowing me to survive the first forty-three years of life. Without the initial life-saving treatment you provided, my life would have been tragically brief.

Thank you to Rebeca Covers for bringing to life the exact book cover I imagined. Thank you to Michal Garret for extensive assistance in editing.

Finally, I am grateful to the reader for allowing me to share my heart with you.

Made in the USA
Columbia, SC
15 January 2018